"New to town or just visiting?" the waitress asked as she handed Ava a menu

"New, actually. I'm a marine biologist at the new Coastal Research Institute. My name's Ava Vincent."

"Nice to meet you, Ava." Instead of leaving, she paused and then said, "I don't mean to be nosy, but you look so familiar. Have you been in before?"

Ava laughed. "No. But you're the second person in the past two days to tell me that."

"You look enough like a friend of ours to be his sister." Someone called her away then, leaving Ava sitting there, her heart pounding. It couldn't be. Her brothers had lived in Dallas. Still, they could have moved. No, better to not get her hopes up. Or her fears.

She opened her newspaper and skimmed the articles until a photo caught her eye. Holding her breath, she spread the paper out to take a more careful look. *Oh, my God, it's him. It's Mark.* Ava didn't need to read the caption to be certain—she knew who he was from the instant she set eyes on him.

Seeing his picture was like looking in a mirror.

Dear Reader,

This story has been in the back of my mind since I wrote the first book in the Brothers Kincaid series, *Trouble in Texas*. Miranda's story—the lost sister's story—was one I didn't know much about at first. I knew she'd run away very young, I knew she hadn't died, but I couldn't imagine why she hadn't tried to find her brothers in the more than twenty years since she'd left home. But Miranda, or Ava as she now calls herself, had a secret she couldn't share with anyone.

Jack Williams isn't running from his past—he's carrying his teenage son with him. Then he meets Ava and for the first time since he lost his wife, he knows there's a woman he could be happy with. But he also knows there's more to Ava than she's sharing. Even with the man who comes to love her.

Remember Texas is about second chances. Who hasn't done something in their past they regret, or even bitterly regret? Ava and Jack discover that love makes these second chances possible.

Hope you enjoy Ava and Jack's journey. I love to hear from readers. E-mail me at eve@evegaddy.net and visit my Web site at www.evegaddy.net. You can also reach me at P.O. Box 131704, Tyler, TX 75713-1704.

Sincerely,

Eve Gaddy

REMEMBER TEXAS
Eve Gaddy

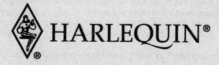

HARLEQUIN®

TORONTO • NEW YORK • LONDON
AMSTERDAM • PARIS • SYDNEY • HAMBURG
STOCKHOLM • ATHENS • TOKYO • MILAN • MADRID
PRAGUE • WARSAW • BUDAPEST • AUCKLAND

ISBN-13: 978-0-373-71367-7
ISBN-10:   0-373-71367-3

REMEMBER TEXAS

Copyright © 2006 by Eve Gaddy.

This edition published by arrangement with Harlequin Books S.A.

® and TM are trademarks of the publisher. Trademarks indicated with
® are registered in the United States Patent and Trademark Office, the
Canadian Trade Marks Office and in other countries.

www.eHarlequin.com

Printed in U.S.A.

ABOUT THE AUTHOR

Eve Gaddy is the award-winning author of fourteen novels. She lives in east Texas with her husband and children and her incredibly spoiled golden retriever, Maverick, who is convinced he's her third child. Besides her family, she loves reading, chocolate, air-conditioning and the Dallas Mavericks. She is currently hard at work on more novels for Harlequin Superromance.

Books by Eve Gaddy

HARLEQUIN SUPERROMANCE

Don't miss any of our special offers. Write to us at the following address for information on our newest releases.

Harlequin Reader Service
U.S.: 3010 Walden Ave., P.O. Box 1325, Buffalo, NY 14269
Canadian: P.O. Box 609, Fort Erie, Ont. L2A 5X3

This one is for my husband, Bob. I love you!

CHAPTER ONE

"COLE, WHAT ARE YOU DOING?" Jack Williams pounded on the closed bedroom door. "I have to leave for work. Come on, I'll drop you at school on my way."

"I'm not going."

His voice was muffled but determined. Jack gritted his teeth and silently counted to ten. "Come on, buddy, you know you have to go. It won't be so bad once you get to know some of the kids."

Cole opened the door and glared at him with eyes the color of whiskey. His mother's eyes, except Cynthia had never looked at Jack with such venom in her gaze. "I don't want to know them. This place sucks. I want to go home."

"Don't start this again. Aransas City is home now. And we don't have time to mess around. You're going to be late, and so am I."

"Like I give a—"

"I'm waiting, Cole," he said, interrupting. "And put on a pair of jeans that fit. Don't forget you're working at the Institute after school."

Cole was a skateboarder and wore baggy pants that always looked like they were one breath away from falling off his butt. Why they never did, Jack didn't know. But he was damned if Cole was wearing those pants to work. At least the T-shirt was one of the milder ones, so they wouldn't have to fight over it as well.

Finally, they were able to leave. Cole hadn't changed his clothes, but Jack blew that defiance off in the interest of getting to work on time. The new research scientist he'd be working with was due at the Institute this morning for her first day, and Jack wanted to arrive before she did.

"I don't see why I have to work at the same place you do," Cole said on the way to school.

"You tried the grocery store and there were no bag boy positions left. It's tough to find a job when you're fifteen. You're lucky Dr. Long hired you." The director had done it as a personal favor to Jack but Jack didn't tell his son that. He thought it would do him good to believe he'd got the job on his own. He might try harder if he did believe it.

"I'm nearly sixteen," Cole said sulkily. "If I had wheels I could work any place I wanted."

"Wheels cost money," Jack said. "Insurance, gas, not to mention the cost of the car itself." He didn't mention he had his eye on a car he intended to give Cole for his birthday in a couple of weeks. It was the next thing to a junker, but he was confident that he could keep it running. And he and Cole could work on it together, which he hoped would bring them closer.

Abandoning the car argument, Cole said, "You don't trust me, that's why you want me there. You're treating me like a baby, wanting to know where I am every minute."

It was an old refrain. But Jack had learned his lesson in Galveston when Cole had fallen in with a bad crowd because his father was working all the time. That was the main reason Jack had decided to move and leave his charter fishing business for something with more regular hours and more free time.

He intended to do better here. He'd be the father Cole needed whether his son liked it or not. "You know what happened in Galveston. If I'm hard on you, you've only yourself to blame. You're going to have to earn back my trust, son."

"I told you, I only smoked weed once. If you hadn't come home early you'd never even have known. We'd still be living in Galveston and not in this nothing town. Why are you making such a big deal out of it?"

"Because it is a big deal. You're lucky it was me who found you and not the police." Besides, he didn't totally buy that that had been the first time the kid had smoked. No, he wasn't that naive, even if he had been too clueless to see the signs before he'd busted his son and his friends.

Cole shrugged, but didn't speak, so Jack continued. "You need to work after school because you need the experience. Not to mention the money."

"Gimme a break. I bet it sucks. It's probably boring as sh—"

"Watch your mouth," Jack said wearily. Thank God they had arrived at the school. "I'll see you later." Luckily, the Institute was only a short walk from the high school. He just hoped Cole showed up and he didn't have to go hunt him down. Not a very good impression to make on the director if that happened.

"I don't feel so good," Cole said, rubbing his stomach. "I think I'm getting the flu or something."

Jack laughed. "Yeah, I'm going to fall for that one." Knowing it would infuriate Cole, he stifled the urge to ruffle his son's hair, as he had when Cole was young. "Better get to class, Cole. I'll see you later."

Cole didn't respond, just got out of the car.

Jack drove the short distance to the Institute and parked his car. As he walked into the building, he was struck again by how new everything looked. But then, since the place had only just opened, it should look new. Some serious money had funded the Coastal Research Institute. Unfortunately, money had become tighter before they'd got around to buying the boats. The director was on the lookout for a big boat that could cruise the gulf for days and sleep several people. But Jack didn't know how long it would be before he found what he wanted.

The boat they did have was a smaller one but still large enough to take care of their initial needs. Though it was older, the *Heart of Texas* was a good, solid thirty-two-foot cruiser and would make a fine research vessel for the bay. It would sleep six, more in a pinch, had a full galley and a decent head. In fact, the boat was great, it just needed a little work, especially on the engine.

Jack's old buddy Mark Kincaid had been instrumental in getting him this job. When Mark had heard Jared Long was looking for a fleet captain, he'd given him Jack's name. Mark had also mentioned the house next to his was for sale, so Jack and Cole had been able to buy it and move right in. Jack definitely owed Mark for all his help.

"Come in, Jack." Jared Long let him into his office and shook hands with a genial smile.

Dr. Long was in his late fifties, a big, balding hulk of a man, and in Jack's opinion, an all-around good guy. The Institute was his baby. He'd founded it, got funding for it and had recruited for it.

"Dr. Vincent is due any minute." He chuckled. "I don't mind telling you we're lucky to get her. She's made quite a name for herself in Florida, with her papers on digital photographic identification of bottlenose dolphins."

"I'm in no hurry," Jack said. "I've been talking to some of the locals about the dolphin population, so I know what areas to start looking in."

"Good. That will help since Dr. Vincent's never been in the area."

"I'd like to thank you again for giving my son a job. He's excited about starting." No reason to let the man know that Cole was being such a pain in the butt.

"Good. I know moving can be hard on kids, especially teenagers."

"Boy, that's the truth"

"How does he like school? Has he made any friends yet?"

Jack shook his head, skipping over the first question. "Not yet. But it's early days. I'm sure he'll make some friends soon." And pray God they weren't into the same things his last group of friends had been involved in.

"Any luck finding someone to help with the engine repair?" Dr. Long asked, changing the subject.

"As a matter of fact, I talked with someone yesterday." Since both he and the director wanted what money the Institute did have to go toward the purchase of more boats, Jack had volunteered to repair the engine himself. Like most charter boat captains, he knew a bit about boat repairs. And what he didn't know he'd planned to get help with. "Mark introduced me to his brother-in-law, Gabe Randolph. Do you know him?"

"Gabe? Sure. He owns the bait and tackle shop under the causeway bridge. Used to be Red's." He laughed and added, "Gabe's really spruced up the place. First time I saw it I couldn't believe the change. Red hadn't done a thing to it in thirty years."

"That's him. He said he'd love to get his hands on a boat engine again. It will have to be in his spare time, but I'm sure we can work something out. He's coming over in the morning, in fact, if I can't get it going by this afternoon."

Someone knocked on the door. "That must be Dr. Vincent," Long said and went to answer it.

"Dr. Vincent, it's wonderful to have you here." He opened the door wider and stepped back.

"Thank you, I'm so happy to be here," a soft, husky voice said.

A woman stepped into the room and every one of Jack's preconceived notions about female scientists exploded into dust. Long, dark sable hair fell to her shoulders in rolling waves. Though she was clearly dressed for work in khaki pants, a sleeveless white blouse and running shoes, the clothes did nothing to hide her incredible body.

"Dr. Ava Vincent, meet Captain Jack Williams. He's our research fleet captain." The director's laugh boomed. "Right now we've only got one vessel, but we intend to add more as soon as we gain more funding. We've got some exciting fund-raisers planned."

Cool blue eyes as deep as the ocean looked him over critically. Her eyes seemed familiar, though he couldn't have said why because he was certain he would have remembered if he'd ever met her. Too self-possessed to be very young, it was hard to tell her exact age. But damn, he could tell one thing for sure. This woman was gorgeous.

"Nice to meet you," she said, and offered him her hand. A woman's hand, soft and feminine, but with a firm, decisive handshake.

"Likewise, Dr. Vincent."

"Please, call me Ava," she said as she dropped his hand. She came farther into the room, took the chair Dr. Long offered her with a soft word of thanks and crossed one leg over the other.

Jack had to remind himself to breathe.

Wow. If she fired his hormones after just one look at her, what was it going to be like to work with her?

Interesting. Very interesting.

CHAPTER TWO

"I WAS JUST TELLING JACK here how lucky we are that you decided to join us," Jared Long said.

"Thank you, but I'm the lucky one, Dr. Long," Ava said, turning her attention away from the fleet captain and back to her new boss. "As you know, there aren't too many places where I could pursue my interest in bottlenose dolphins." Particularly her interest in digital photo identification. How could she turn down the job, especially when Dr. Long had offered to put her in charge of that aspect of the study?

"Please, we're informal around here. Call me Jared."

She glanced at Jack Williams. She wasn't sure what to think of him. He hadn't said much, just looked at her almost blankly. He wasn't un-friendly, exactly, but he sure wasn't as welcoming as Dr. Long had been.

Jack Williams was what her former students would have termed a hottie. Sandy-brown hair, worn a little long, reached the collar of a short-sleeved white T-shirt that showed off tanned, muscular arms. His lean, handsome face hadn't seen a razor for days, but on him it looked good.

But his eyes were what really caught her attention. He had the most vivid green eyes she'd ever seen.

"Any luck finding a place to live?" the director asked. "I know how impossible it is to find a rental in Aransas City."

With a start she realized Jared was talking again. It wouldn't do to let that unwelcome spark of attraction to the boat captain interfere with her job. "I'm closing on a house this weekend. Friday, actually." Which was a huge step, considering until she'd been offered this dream job she hadn't planned on ever coming back to Texas, much less living here again. No, she'd hightailed it out of the state more than twenty years before, and had vowed never to set foot in it again.

"I'm sure you're anxious to get acquainted with the rest of the staff and see your office. Let me show you around." As they all stood, Jared laughed and added, "I know you're champing at the bit to get to work on that engine, Jack. We won't keep you any longer."

"All right. See you later. Nice to meet you, Ava," he said, shaking her hand again.

"Is there a chance we can go over the schedule later this afternoon?" she asked before he could leave.

"Sure. I'll be at the boat." He nodded to her and the director and left quickly.

After Jared gave her a tour of the facilities, they went to her office. He opened the door and said in a justifiably proud tone, "All state-of-the-art equipment. Your computer is supposed to have all the bells and whistles." He reeled off the specifications in the cheerful jargon of one who knows and appreciates electronics.

She barely stopped herself from reverently stroking the seventeen-inch flat-screen monitor. The new computer was clearly head and shoulders above the desktop she'd been using at her previous job. "That's great. I'll load FinScan on it as soon as I get a bit settled."

"Well, I'll leave you to it. Just give me a call if you need anything."

Ava spent the remainder of the morning putting her office in order. Everything in it was brand-new, and, to Ava, a little intimidating. Empty bookshelves waiting to be filled. A gleaming wood desk that was clean save for the computer and a cordless phone. She'd like it better once her desk was covered with notes and files. She liked the lived-in look.

First, she arranged her research. She put the articles and papers in the file cabinet, arranged the books and magazines—mostly marine mammal publications—on the shelves.

Among other equipment, she had access to a waterproof digital camera, so she spent some time familiarizing herself with it as well.

While she did this she thought about her meeting earlier that morning. Dr. Long—Jared—had been much as she'd expected from her phone conversations with him, and she knew she was going to really enjoy working at the Institute.

She'd be spending a lot more time with Jack Williams, though, than the director. She wasn't sure how she felt about that, given her instant attraction to the man. She hoped he was married. That would make it easier to resist any unwelcome sparks. Which she fully intended to do.

Late that afternoon she went to find Jack and discuss their schedule for the next few days. She really wanted a chance to take a preliminary tour of the bay, become more familiar with it. Although she'd lived in Texas as a child, she'd never been near the Texas coast.

Looking for Jack, Ava headed out to the dock where the *Heart of Texas* was moored. Sure enough, he was there, with the engine compartment open, a tool in hand and cussing a blue streak.

"Son of a bitch!" he said, among other things.

"Captain?"

He didn't look up but continued fooling with the motor. Ava was given ample opportunity to study his backside, encased in old, tight, faded jeans and a T-shirt that proclaimed, Don't Worry, Go Fishing. She cleared her throat and tried again. "Jack," she said, louder and more firmly. "I need to talk to you."

He looked up then. He'd tied a red bandana around his forehead to keep his hair out of his face. A face now liberally streaked with grease and dirt.

His eyes snapped with impatience. "What about?"

"Our schedule. Remember?"

He muttered something, then went back to the engine. It didn't seem to dawn on him that she was technically his boss. Or at least, his superior.

"I need to talk to you about our schedule," she repeated.

"Schedule? We don't have one." He spoke to the engine, not to her.

Annoyed by now, she said with what she considered admirable restraint, "What do you mean, we don't have one? Isn't it part of your job description to take me out on the bay? And if it's not your job, whose is it?"

He grunted as he wrestled some more with the motor. "Yeah, yeah. But nobody's going anywhere if I can't get this sucker fixed," he said, his back still to her. "Do something useful and hand me that crescent wrench."

Instead of irritating her, the command amused her. Clearly, here was a man who didn't cater to anyone. She climbed down into the boat and looked at the assortment of tools in the chest. Since she didn't have a clue what a crescent wrench was, she picked up a tool at random and slapped it into his open palm, hard.

He grunted something that might have been thanks, started to use the tool, then glanced over his shoulder at her, pinning her with a sharp look. "This isn't a crescent wrench. It's not even a wrench."

"And I'm not your assistant," she said, her tone deliberately mild.

He stared at her a minute before a reluctant grin transformed his face. The smile made him look younger, even more handsome and...oh, hell, hot.

He turned all the way around and leaned back against the engine, wiping his arm across his forehead as he did so. "Sorry. I'm a little frustrated. I've been trying to fix this for most of the day and getting nowhere. There's not much point in talking about a schedule until the engine is fixed."

"I had hoped we could have taken a preliminary circuit of the bay, but I guess that's out of the question today. I didn't realize the boat was out of commission. I thought it was new."

"Not hardly," he said with a laugh. "Our budget doesn't run to a brand-new research vessel."

She supposed that wasn't a shock. After all, she'd been amazed at the depth of funding as it was. According to Jared, much of it had come through private donations. Unfortunately, a good research vessel was a requirement, not a luxury. "Do you have any idea how long it will take to fix it?" Because until she had access to the boat she couldn't begin to identify the dolphins.

"A friend of mine's coming to help me in the morning. With luck, by tomorrow afternoon we'll have it working. I hope." He pulled another bandana out of his pocket and wiped his face, then looked at her closely, frowning. "Have we met before?"

"No. Why?"

"You look familiar. Are you sure we've never met?"

Ava laughed. "Can't you do better than that?"

"It's not a line. You really do look familiar. I think it's your eyes."

"They're blue," she said drily. "Lots of people have blue eyes."

He rubbed his nose, spreading more grease. "Not like yours, they don't. But if you say we've never met I guess I have to believe you." He turned back to the engine, did something with another tool. "Hot tamale with *chile con queso* on top, I think I've done it—"

Ava stepped forward just in time to receive a chestful of motor oil. At the same time, Jack jumped backward, crashing into her. Her feet slipped out from under her and she grabbed his arm for balance. They both went down in a tangle of arms, legs and heavy-duty motor oil.

She could barely breathe. He weighed a ton. "Get off me!" she managed to squeeze out. She shoved at him ineffectually until a moment later he lifted himself off her and rolled onto his back.

Ava sat up, grateful that at least the oil had stopped spewing. Viscous, black liquid lay in small pools on the once-white deck. Arm flung across his eyes, Jack laughed, a deep, male sound of pure amusement.

She wanted to kill him. "There's nothing funny about this."

He sat up and grinned at her. "Oh, that's where you're wrong. If you could see your face—"

Touching a hand to her cheek, she realized the oil had splattered her face as well as covered her clothes. "What did you think you were doing?" She looked down at her shirt, now liberally streaked with black and gray. Totally shot. No dry cleaner in the universe would be able to get out that kind of stain. "I had to wear my favorite shirt," she muttered.

"I was trying to fix the engine." He got to his feet and held out a hand. "Come on, let me help you up."

"Ha. Forget it." She scrambled to her feet with as much dignity as she could muster.

Which wasn't much because she slipped again and had to grab hold of the side of the boat to keep from falling. Looking down at her feet, she realized her shoes, a brand-new pair of air-soled running shoes, were a lost cause as well.

"Look, I'm sorry," Jack said. "It was an accident." His lips quivered but he controlled the smile, luckily for him. He was just about on her last nerve.

"How about I—" He broke off as the cell phone clipped to his belt rang.

Or at least, she assumed the sound of the Stones' *Satisfaction* was a ring tone and not a radio or CD player suddenly gone berserk.

Frowning at the phone display, he said, "Sorry, I have to take this." He flipped it open. "Yeah, Williams here." He listened intently for a moment. "Are you sure he's— He can't— No. No, I understand. I'll be right there."

After he hung up he cussed under his breath, then stood for a moment, looking grim and staring out at the water. Then he shook his head, closed the engine compartment and started gathering all the tools together and tossing them into the open tool box.

It dawned on her he was leaving. "Are you

crazy? You can't just go off and leave the boat in this shape. It's a disaster."

He glanced at her as he chucked the last tool in and closed the lid. "It'll keep until I can get back to clean up. I'll talk to you later. Right now, I have to go."

She parked her hands on her hips and stared at him incredulously. "What can possibly be so important that you'd leave the boat in a mess like this?"

He'd climbed out of the boat by now and stood on the dock looking down at her. A wry smile twisted his mouth. "My son. That was his school calling to tell me he's sick. We'll talk tomorrow, okay?" Moments later, he was gone.

His son? So he was married. Be careful what you wish for, she thought. To be honest, she was a tiny bit disappointed. Which was absurd, since it was Jack Williams's fault she was standing on the deck of a nasty, dirty boat in the ruins of what was once her favorite white shirt and her newest pair of running shoes.

She looked around, spying a mop and bucket in the corner of the deck. The man had rushed off to pick up his sick son. Though she tried to keep it under wraps, Ava had a soft spot for a man who'd drop everything to take care of his child. She sighed and removed her shoes, setting them on the dock. She couldn't make the boat spotless, but she could clean up the worst of the mess. Jack could do the rest tomorrow.

And, she thought philosophically, Jack Williams would definitely owe her for this. Which could only help, all things considered.

IT DIDN'T TAKE LONG to reach the high school, but by the time Jack arrived there he was seething. He didn't for a minute believe Cole was sick. This was his son's passive-aggressive way of getting out of work. But the nurse had been adamant that Jack needed to pick Cole up, so here he was.

Once Jack had heard the words *no fever* he hadn't paid close attention to what else the nurse had said. He had to admit, Cole was playing it for all he was worth, clutching his stomach and moaning in pain as he lay on the cot in the nurse's office. If Jack didn't know better he might have bought the act as much as the nurse appeared to.

But he did know better. Still, he didn't say anything on the way home, preferring to wait and give his full attention to reading his son the riot act. Not that Jack expected a lecture to do much good, but he had to try.

They pulled into the drive and Cole sprang out to rush inside. Jack caught up to him before he could bound up the stairs and disappear into his room. "Where do you think you're going?"

Cole stopped with his hand on the banister and stared at him. "To my room."

"No, you're not. You're going out and pull weeds until it's time to go to work. You may have fooled the school nurse but it's not working with me."

"Dad, I'm not lying. I feel like I'm gonna barf."

"Yeah? Well, you can barf outside."

Jack felt a momentary qualm at the sight of his son's woebegone face. But he squelched it quickly. Cole had taken advantage of Jack's soft heart too many times to count.

"Please don't make me, Dad. I feel really sick." He curved his arm over his stomach and looked pitiful.

So pitiful Jack nearly relented. Instead he walked over to Cole and put his hand on his shoulder. "Outside, Cole, now. The weeds are waiting."

Cole let go of the banister, took a step forward and threw up all over Jack's shoes.

Oh, shit, Jack thought as he helped him to the bathroom. *Wouldn't you know he'd be telling the truth the day I decided to get tough?*

CHAPTER THREE

IT TOOK JACK A WHILE to get Cole settled in bed. He left the phone within easy reach and a bucket beside the bed in case of emergency. After he cleaned up the mess downstairs, there was another one waiting for him at the Institute. He didn't like leaving his son, but he hoped the boy would sleep most of the time he was gone. Besides, if he didn't clean up the boat tonight it would be almost impossible to clean by the next day.

And, though he didn't like imposing on her, he called Mark's wife, Cat, to ask if Cole could call her if he needed to. She said she'd be happy to check on Cole. Jack hated to ask her since she had her hands full with two young kids and another due in a few months, but he didn't have much choice.

At the Institute, Jack walked up to the boat and did a double take. While not gleaming and spotless, all traces of the oil were gone. The only person he could imagine cleaning it was Milton, the janitor. That seemed odd, though, since Milton had already stated that his job didn't extend to cleaning the boat. Jack did the rest of the cleanup quickly, then went in search of the janitor to thank him.

"I didn't do it," Milton said. "I didn't even know there was a problem. The boat's not my responsibility, you know." He glared at Jack as if expecting him to give him a hard time.

"I know it's not," Jack assured him hastily. "That's why—" He broke off and ran a hand through his hair. "If you didn't do it, who did?"

"Beats me." Milton shrugged and went back to work.

There was only one person who could have done it. Dr. Vincent. Oh, man, he felt bad enough that he'd ruined her clothes. Then he'd laughed. The fact that she'd cleaned the boat made him feel that much worse. He wondered if that's why she'd done it, or was she simply that nice?

Tomorrow he'd offer to pay to have her clothes cleaned, or replaced, more likely. In the meantime, he was simply grateful she'd done it, whatever her reasons.

By the time he got back home, Cole was awake and hungry, so he fed him soup and crackers that thankfully stayed down. Cole went back to bed and Jack sat down to watch a baseball game. He was trying to decide what he wanted for dinner when his doorbell rang.

"Hey," Mark said, handing him a large pot. "Cat sent this over. She said Cole was sick."

"Thanks. Come on in." He took the pot to the kitchen and set it on the stove. "Cole's eaten. I fed him early. But I'm hungry." He took the lid off and sniffed. He nearly moaned as the mouth-watering aroma of homemade chicken noodle soup hit his nostrils. "That smells incredible. Cat didn't have to cook for us."

Mark shrugged. "She loves to cook. Just eat it and be grateful."

"Trust me, I am. Help yourself to a beer," he said, getting out a bowl and spoon for the soup.

"Sounds good." Mark went to the refrigerator and pulled out a can. "Want one?"

"I better not. I think Cole's okay now but you never can tell with kids and viruses."

"Tell me about it," Mark said, popping the top of his beer can and taking a seat at the table. "One of my worst memories was the time both the kids and Cat had it. It nearly killed me taking care of them. If one wasn't throwing up the other was. And little kids never make it to the bathroom."

Jack laughed, thinking of that afternoon. "Neither do big kids sometimes." He ate some soup, then put his spoon down and rubbed the back of his neck. "Cole told me he was sick, but I didn't believe him. I feel like a jerk. Poor kid."

"Why didn't you believe him? Has he faked being sick before?"

Picking up his spoon again, Jack nodded. "All the time when we lived in Galveston. He doesn't much like school."

"Then it shouldn't have surprised him if you didn't believe him this time."

True, but Jack still felt bad about the whole thing. He started eating again. Homemade chicken noodle soup tasted nothing like the canned stuff. Jack's wife used to make soup from scratch, but honesty made him admit hers wasn't as good as what he was eating now. "This soup is amazing. Thank Cat for me."

"I will. She's a great cook, isn't she?"

"Yeah, she is. Is that why you married her?"

Mark laughed. "No, but it's a nice bonus." He took a sip of beer, then said, "We're having a barbecue Sunday afternoon. Why don't you come, bring Cole? There'll be a lot of kids, probably some close to his age."

"Thanks. We will."

"And if you want to bring a date, that's fine too."

Jack laughed and set down his spoon. "That's not happening. I haven't had a date in—" He broke off because Ava Vincent's face popped into his mind. He didn't know why, though, since after this morning she wasn't likely to go out with him even if he did ask her.

"What?"

Jack looked at Mark. "Nothing. It's just— I met a woman today. The new research scientist."

"So spill. Is she hot?"

"Oh, yeah. She's awesome." He nodded. Dark hair. Deep blue eyes, like the ocean. He glanced at Mark again. Eyes that looked like… "But that's not it. I kept thinking I'd met her before." Then it dawned on him. "The weird thing is, she looks like you."

"Right." Mark laughed and set down his beer.

"No, I'm telling you, that's why she seemed so familiar to me. She could be your sister."

Mark's expression went from amused to grim in the space of seconds. "Not funny."

"I wasn't trying to be funny. I'm not kidding, Mark. She looks enough like you to be your sister."

Mark stared at him for a long moment, then closed his eyes and cursed.

"What's wrong?" Mark looked sick but Jack couldn't understand why. He'd known Mark for years, had met his two younger brothers, Jay and Brian, whom he knew Mark had raised. In fact, Jay lived in Aransas City now, too, and was married to Mark's sister-in-law. In all the years he'd known Mark, Jack had never heard anything about…a sister? But there was only one reason Mark would be looking as upset as he was.

"Oh, my God, you have a sister?"

He opened his eyes and gave Jack a look brimming with pain. "Had. She ran away from home when she was fifteen. No one's seen her since."

Jack gazed at him, open-mouthed. "God, I'm sorry, Mark. I had no idea."

"There's no way you could have known. It's not something I talk about. I looked for her for years, had private investigators looking, too. So did my mother. Nothing. No one ever turned up even a hint of what happened to her."

"What was her name?"

"Miranda."

The name of Mark's youngest child. "You named your daughter after her."

Mark gave a jerky nod.

"Do you think…maybe you should see this woman. Her name is Ava Vincent, but she could have changed it. I'm telling you, the resemblance is so strong—"

"I don't need to see her," Mark said harshly. "I'm not going down that road again. Hoping, praying, getting disappointed again and again, wishing for anything, just a tiny crumb of information."

He shook his head. "No. My hope died a long time ago, just like she did." Gripping his hands together, he said, "My sister is dead. She vanished without a trace more than twenty years ago. Do you really think she'd show up out of the blue in Aransas City?"

No, he honestly didn't. "Yeah, you're right. I guess the resemblance is just a coincidence. Look, I'm sorry I ever brought it up."

"It's all right." Mark sucked in a breath, visibly trying to gain control of himself. "Like I said, it's not your fault." He got up and tossed his can in the trash. "Don't forget about Sunday."

"We'll be there." Jack walked him to the door. "Thanks again for the soup." He wanted to say something but he couldn't think what. So he didn't say anything more, figuring he'd stuck his foot in it plenty already.

"No problem."

Jack watched Mark leave and cursed himself silently. He'd screwed up three for three today. His son, his new colleague, and his best friend. *Way to go, Jack.* Thank God the day was almost over. Even he couldn't manage to offend anyone else that night, especially since he intended to go straight to bed.

WHEN AVA ARRIVED AT WORK the next morning she found Jack Williams waiting outside her office door, leaning against the wall with a newspaper tucked under his arm.

"Hi. How's your son?" she asked as she opened the door and he followed her inside.

"Better, thanks. He's home today but I think it was just a twenty-four-hour bug. He should be able to go back to school tomorrow. And to work. Jared gave him a job here as a gofer after school."

"That's good. I'm glad he's all right." She took a sip of the coffee she'd brought with her from the lounge. "So, what can I do for you?"

Looking uncomfortable, he shifted. "Other way around. I wanted to pay your cleaning bill. And, uh—" He hesitated and she thought if he'd been wearing a collared shirt and tie he'd have been tugging on it. "I want to apologize for laughing."

Willing to let bygones be bygones, she shrugged. "Oh, that. I guess it was kind of funny with all that oil going everywhere. Not that I thought so yesterday."

"You had every right to be mad as hell at me. Which is why I don't understand why you cleaned up the boat. You did, didn't you?"

Ava waved a hand and leaned back against her desk. "Call it a goodwill gesture. You had more important things on your mind."

"Yeah. When you're a single parent you get used to juggling everything in your life. When the school called I didn't have much choice except to go pick him up."

So he wasn't married after all. "Divorce is hard," she said. "Especially when you have kids, I imagine. I don't have any but that's what I've heard." She hadn't found her divorce hard, either, but she knew most people did. You'd think she would have been more upset, especially considering Paul had left her for another woman, but she'd been more relieved than angry. And she hadn't been tempted since.

"I'm not divorced. My wife died six years ago."

"I'm sorry."

"Yeah, me too. But about that cleaning bill—"

"Don't worry about it. The clothes are a loss, I'm afraid, but they weren't expensive."

"Still, the whole thing was my responsibility. Let me pay to replace them."

Judging by the set of his jaw, he wasn't going to give in on the issue, so she capitulated rather than continue arguing. Besides, he was right. He did owe her new clothes. But she'd take pity on him and not make him pay for the shoes too. She could see he hadn't even thought about that. "All right. I'll let you know when I find something to replace them. Is there anything else?"

"My friend is coming over this morning to help with the engine. With any luck, by this afternoon I can take you out on the bay."

"That's great."

"I'll give you a call when I know more." He laid the folded newspaper down on her desk. "Thought you might like to look through the local paper. The

Aransas Bay *Port o' Call.* Cole and I just recently moved here, too, and I've gotten a kick out of reading it. It gives you some information about the area, local activities and stuff like that. The gossip column is a hoot, even when you don't know anyone."

"Thanks. I'll do that." Jack Williams was turning out to be a lot more thoughtful than she'd have believed yesterday.

He left shortly after that and Ava settled down to get some work done. At lunchtime she decided to try the Scarlet Parrot, a waterfront bar and grill that Jared had told her about. She took the paper with her to read because she'd be eating alone.

The hostess, a very pretty, obviously pregnant brunette, seated her. "New to town or just visiting?" she asked as she handed Ava a menu.

"New, actually. I'm a marine biologist at the new Coastal Research Institute."

"Ah, Jared sent you then. Welcome to Aransas City."

"Thanks. Yes, Jared says this is one of his favorite restaurants. I'm Ava Vincent."

"Nice to meet you, Ava. I'm Delilah Randolph. My husband Cam and I own the restaurant." But instead of leaving, she said, "I don't mean to be rude or nosy, but you look so familiar. Have you been in before?"

Ava laughed. "No. But you're the second person in the past two days to tell me that. The other was a man and I thought he was giving me a line."

Delilah laughed and placed a hand on her rounded belly. "I promise, I'm not trying to pick you up. But you look enough like a friend of ours to be his sister. He's my husband's brother-in-law, actually."

Someone called her away then, leaving Ava sitting there, her heart pounding. No, it couldn't be. Her brothers had lived in Dallas. Still, they could have moved.

Wait a minute. She remembered now, they'd had an uncle who lived here. She hadn't thought about him in years. He was bound to have passed away by now. Even if he was still alive, though, that didn't mean that any of the rest of the family would be in town. No, better to not get her hopes up. Or her fears.

After she gave the waitress her order she opened the paper, skimming it at first. She skipped over the gossip column, intending to read it later because Jack had recommended it.

Flipping through the articles, her gaze caught

on a headline: Copper's Cove Wild Bird Sanctuary Garners National Attention. She started to read the article, then glanced at the picture beneath the headline and her heart nearly stopped.

Holding her breath, she spread the paper out to take a more careful look. She barely glanced at the petite brunette. Her attention was all for the man standing beside the woman, smiling at her with obvious pride.

Oh, my God, it's him. It's Mark. Ava didn't need to read the caption to be certain, she'd known who he was from the instant she'd set eyes on him. Seeing his picture had been like looking in the mirror.

CHAPTER FOUR

AVA QUICKLY SCANNED the caption under the picture: "Cat Kincaid, founder of Copper's Cove Wild Bird sanctuary, and her husband, Mark, of Aransas City."

Mark lived here, right here in the same town she did. With his wife and…children? Did he have children? His wife was clearly pregnant. Ava might have nieces and nephews.

"'Scuse me. Here's your food, ma'am."

Ava looked up. The young waitress held a plate and smacked her gum, clearly impatient with Ava for having the newspaper spread out over the table. She moved the paper aside, relieved when the girl set down the plate and left. She went back to the article to pore over it, letting her food grow cold. Cat had just accepted another donation that would, she was quoted as saying, allow them to hire a small paid staff to be supplemented by volunteers. She read that the sanctuary had opened several years before and that Mark, a Fish and Wildlife Service agent, had also had a hand in the creation of the sanctuary.

So Mark had achieved his career goal. He'd wanted to work with the FWS as long as she could remember. And he was doing it here, in Aransas City. Impossible, but true.

Ava barely remembered eating or paying or getting from the restaurant to the Institute. But when she opened the car door and the heat swamped her, she started feeling again, thinking again. She got out and went straight to the air-conditioned office.

"Can I borrow a phone book?"

"Sure. Here you go." Raney Cooper, the receptionist, handed her the small book.

Ava reached for it, noticing her hand was shaking. She grabbed the book, pulling it to her chest and clenching both hands around it.

Raney paused and looked at her more closely. "Are you all right? You look a little pale. The stomach flu is going around, you know."

"I'm fine. Thanks for asking." No doubt she looked as if she'd seen a ghost. Essentially, she had.

She walked quickly to her office and locked the door behind her. Opening the phone book, she leafed frantically to the *K*'s. There he was, listed with his wife: "Kincaid, Mark and Cat." Letting out a shaky breath, she made a note of the address and phone number, then realized the line above Mark's read Kincaid, Jason M.D.

It had to be Jay. Oh, lord, her little brother was here, too. And Jay was a doctor. How could that be? In her mind he was still seven years old.

There was no mention of Brian, her youngest brother, so she assumed he didn't live in Aransas City, unless he was unlisted. But at least two of her three brothers did.

And now so did she. What was she going to do? She couldn't avoid them, not in a town this size. Besides, she didn't want to avoid them. Now that she knew where they were she wanted desperately to see them. She could feel tears burning behind her eyelids at the thought of her brothers being so close. After all this time, they were close enough to talk to, to touch…to hug.

Guilt crushed her in a viselike grip. It had been her choice not to contact them, her choice to let the relationship die. Would they even want to see her? After she'd disappeared from their lives so completely and for so long?

Her parents—they were a completely different

matter. She wouldn't cross the street to see her father. She'd run the other way rather than face him again, even after all these years. Her feelings about her mother were a little more complicated. Her mother had let her children down. Especially Ava. Lillian hadn't been there when Ava had desperately needed her. That last night…God, no, she wouldn't think about that now. She'd think about her brothers instead.

She'd loved her brothers. Had never stopped loving them, missing them. If she were honest with herself, she'd admit that finding her brothers again had been on her mind for years, and when she'd been offered the job in Aransas City she'd fantasized about finding them, hoping they'd still be living in Texas. But she hadn't expected to find them here, in the same small town she'd ended up in. Coincidence? No, she didn't believe in coincidence. More like fate.

But none of those feelings changed her dilemma. What could she say to them, when they asked, as they were bound to, why she'd never tried to find them after they'd all grown up? Why she'd disappeared from their lives and never sent them so much as a Christmas card in the more than twenty years since?

She couldn't tell them about a past so reprehensible she could never think of it without feeling shame and disgust. Couldn't remember it without that intense feeling of self-hatred.

Her phone rang. She thought about ignoring it, but anything was better than reliving her past. "Ava Vincent," she said automatically, though a tiny voice in her mind whispered, *Miranda Kincaid.*

"Great news," a deep male voice said. "I've got the boat working."

What boat? And who the— She shook her head, clearing the jumble of thoughts. "Jack?"

"At your service. When will you be ready to go? We won't be able to do more than make a quick circuit of the bay, but that should be enough to give you an idea of how you want to start the study and make you a little more familiar with the area."

Focus, she told herself. *You can't afford to think about your brothers, not yet.* When she got home tonight, she'd figure out what to do. Or rather, how to do it.

"Give me half an hour," she said, hoping she could pull herself together by then.

"So, what do you think?" Jack asked Ava. They'd been cruising around for over an hour, hugging the shoreline, and she'd yet to say more than two words to him. He didn't think she was mad at him. No, she wasn't mad, but she'd been...he thought about it some more and settled on *distracted*.

As he'd expected, she'd snapped multiple pictures of dolphins, but for reasons he couldn't put his finger on her heart didn't seem to be in it. It was almost as if she took no pleasure from it, which didn't jibe with what he knew about her professionally. And as far as he knew, this was her first outing in Aransas Bay. He'd expected at least a little enthusiasm. She was outside, on the water, taking pictures for her study. She should have been in dolphin heaven.

She lowered the camera and looked at him. "What do I think about what?"

He gestured. "The boat, the bay, the weather. Who's going to the World Series. You know, conversation? You've heard of the concept, right?" He didn't know about her, but he didn't want to go out day after day and never talk.

She stared at him a minute. "I guess I've been a little distracted. Sorry."

"Yeah, I noticed. Anything you want to talk about?"

She shook her head. "It's nothing." She put a hand to her temple and rubbed. "A headache."

He wasn't too sure of that but he let it go. "Are you always this quiet?"

"No." She smiled and added, "The boat is great, Aransas Bay is a lot different from where I worked in Florida, the heat is brutal, and I don't follow baseball. Basketball's my game. How about those Mavericks? Any other questions?"

He grinned. "A few. I've never been to Florida. Tell me why it's so different."

"I worked at a marine science institute in the Keys. It was gorgeous. The beaches are white sand, the blue water is close in." She paused, considering. "It's prettier, but...the Texas coast has its own appeal. It's more—" she lifted a shoulder "—rugged than Florida, I think."

"We don't have pristine resort-type beaches, that's for sure. But I've always liked the Texas coast."

"This is my first time out on the bay," she said, confirming his suspicions. "I like it."

"Good, because you'll be seeing a lot of it. Ready to call it a day? We can go over our plan for the next few weeks if you want. Seems like we should have an idea of which areas we want

to explore instead of just cruising around aim-
lessly. I've been talking to some locals, so I do
have some thoughts about that."

"That sounds like a good idea. I won't need to
go out every day, since I'll need to build in some
time to identify the dolphins by the dorsal fins I
photograph. Unfortunately, not all of the photos
are in digital format and online so I have to look
through analog albums as well." She put her
camera down and looked at him for the first time
since they'd left. "I haven't seen that many
dolphins today. I hope that's not a bad sign."

"Nah. Some days they're everywhere, some
days they're hard to find."

She paused for a moment, then said, "Do you
know a place called Copper's Cove? It's the site
of a bird sanctuary."

He shot her a surprised glance. "Where'd you
hear about that? It's not exactly national news."

"I read about it in the local paper. The one you
gave me this morning. And according to them, it
is national news now. They've just been given a
large grant."

He'd forgotten he'd given her the *Port o' Call*.
"Can you beat that? Yeah, I know where it is. Do
you want to go there? It's a cool place, but I don't

know if you're likely to find dolphins in those waters. It's awfully shallow."

"Do you mind? Is it out of the way?"

"No, it's not far from the Institute. We're headed that way anyway."

"Thank you. So tell me, do you...know the woman who founded it?"

She'd tried to come across as nonchalant, but he thought she sounded tense. He rubbed his nose and gave her another considering look. "Yeah, actually, I do. Cat Kincaid is my next-door neighbor. Married to a friend of mine, Mark Kincaid." He thought it odd that she hadn't voluntarily said much until she started pumping him about the sanctuary.

"Mark's the reason I'm here," he continued. "When he heard Dr. Long was looking for a captain, he gave him my name."

"That was nice of him."

"Yeah, he's a nice guy. He and Cat are both nice." He shot her a curious glance. "Are you interested in birds as well as dolphins?"

"I used to be. It's been a long time, though. I've spent a lot of time learning about marine mammals and haven't had a chance to do anything with my birding interests."

"You should let me introduce you to Cat, then. She's into birds. Rehabs them." He paused a moment and added, "Funny thing—" he watched her closely as he said it "—Mark's the reason I thought I'd met you before."

She'd been looking out at the bay but at that she turned to him. "I don't understand."

Since they were nearing the cove, he slowed down. "You look like him. Kind of spooky, how much you look like him. I don't suppose you have family in the area?"

She was silent for a long moment, then said, "No, I—I don't have any family period."

Then why are you so interested in the Kincaids? he thought. But maybe he was making too much of it. She could simply be curious, as she'd said, and her resemblance to Mark was a fluke. Mark had certainly thought so.

But Mark hadn't seen her.

He should leave it alone. Mark wouldn't thank him for bringing up the topic of his sister again. He'd told Jack in no uncertain terms to forget it, and it wasn't any of his business. Besides, Ava had seen the picture. If she really was Mark's sister, then it was up to her to do something about it.

"Speaking of family," she asked, "how old is your son?"

"Fifteen. Nearly sixteen."

She studied him a minute. "You don't look old enough to have a child that age."

He laughed. "Thanks, but sometimes I feel like I'm a hundred when I'm dealing with him."

"Is he interested in boats, like you are?"

"No. Right now the only thing he's interested in is going back to Galveston. That's where we moved from."

"It must be hard raising him alone."

"You can say that again. I wonder—" He stopped.

"What?" she prompted.

He shook his head. "I don't want to bore you with my childrearing problems."

"I'm not bored. What were you going to say?"

She sounded sincerely interested so he went ahead and said it. "I just wondered how different things would be if Cynthia was still here. She was a great mother. Always knew what to do." He laughed without much humor. "I don't, to say the least." No, Jack continually felt as if he were swimming in quicksand.

"When did you lose her?"

"Six years ago. Car wreck. One minute she was here, the next she was gone."

"I'm so sorry."

"Yeah, me, too. But enough of my life story. There's Copper's Cove right ahead of us."

"It's beautiful," she said.

She was quiet after that and Jack didn't attempt more conversation. Something was going on with her, but he couldn't figure out what.

A short time later they pulled up to the dock. He helped Ava out of the boat, then yielded to the impulse he'd had since he first saw her. "Would you like to grab some dinner after work? I have to pick up Cole later, but we could catch a quick bite somewhere."

She looked surprised. "That sounds nice but I'd better not. There's something I have to do tonight."

"Okay. Maybe a rain check?"

She smiled but didn't answer. Then she headed inside.

He stared after her for a long moment. Talk about a killer smile. He wondered what it meant. She was the first woman in a long time he'd really wanted to go out with. He'd been so caught up in raising his son, he just hadn't made time for women.

Ava Vincent was worth making time for, though.

CHAPTER FIVE

"WANT ME TO FIX grilled cheese for dinner?" Jack asked Cole after he picked him up from the Institute and brought him home. The sandwich was one of Cole's favorites. He wasn't much of a cook, but after Cynthia had died he hadn't had a choice but to learn. He usually went for simple meals, though he could make a mean spaghetti and meat sauce.

"Okay."

Instead of hanging out in the kitchen as he once would have done, Cole retreated to his room. Jack sighed.

A short time later he called Cole in and they sat down to sandwiches, chips and milk. Not the greatest meal but far from the worst. He watched Cole eat for a minute, then said, "So, tell me about work. Did you enjoy it? What do you think about the Institute?"

Cole shrugged. "It was okay." He stuffed some more food in his mouth.

When he'd been little Cole had talked nonstop. Not anymore. "What did they have you do?"

He rolled his eyes but answered. "Clean up stuff, file stuff."

Jack waited a bit, then prompted. "Is that all?"

Showing more animation than he had yet, Cole shook his head. "Dr. Long showed me the dolphin tank and said when we had one to rehab I could help with it. Sometimes they need twenty-four-hour help, he said, and you can only do a four-hour shift. So they go through a lot of volunteers. He said I could get in the tank with the dolphins and everything." He sent Jack a challenging look as if he expected an argument.

"That sounds like fun," was all Jack said. Jared had already discussed the possibility with Jack, but he didn't tell Cole that. Sometimes getting the kid to talk was exhausting, he thought. "How was school?"

"Okay."

Looked like they were back to one-word answers. Jack gritted his teeth. "Have you met anyone you like yet?"

"A couple of guys. They invited me to a party Friday night."

"That's great." An unwelcome thought occurred to him. "Will the parents be there?"

Cole rolled his eyes again. "I guess."

"Find out and you can go."

Cole shot him a disgusted look. "I'm not asking them that. I'll look like a dork."

"No parents, no party."

"Forget it, then." He got up and took his plate to the sink, rinsed it off and put it in the dishwasher. Jack had drilled that into his head often enough that it was automatic. "You don't want me to have a life."

Jack heard the frustration in his voice, which made him answer more patiently than he might have. "Yes, I do. I just don't want you to get in trouble. I'm sure you can figure out a way to find out if the parents will be there without looking like a dork."

Cole didn't answer and left the room. Jack cleaned up the dinner dishes and wished he didn't have to be such a hard-ass with his son. But he just didn't see any way around it. The plain truth was, he didn't trust Cole not to get in trouble at a party with no parents around.

He found Cole in the living room parked in

front of the TV. "I'm going to run over to Mark's for a little while. Don't forget to do your homework." He took Cole's grunt as a sign of agreement.

He walked across the yard in the gathering twilight. Although it was October, it was still hotter than Hades most of the time, but Jack didn't really mind that. He was used to it. What he did mind was the struggle to get through to his son. There had to be a way of getting close to Cole again, but he wasn't sure he'd ever find it.

As he reached his neighbor's door, Jack heard shrieking, but he went ahead and knocked. Noise wasn't unusual in the Kincaid household, he'd quickly discovered.

Mark answered the door holding his two-year-old daughter, who giggled and patted her father's cheek. "Story," she demanded.

"In a minute, sweetheart," he told her. "Hey, Jack, what's up?"

"Not much. I had a favor to ask you, but it looks like you're busy."

"No, no, come on in." He waved at the couch. "It's Cat's turn to read, anyway."

"Want Daddy," Miranda said, pursing her lips and planting a smacking kiss on Mark's cheek.

Mark's little girl really was his spitting image, with her dark hair and amazingly blue eyes. He reminded himself not to bring up the fact that those eyes looked exactly like Ava Vincent's, too.

"Let's go see Mommy," Mark said, and carried the child out of the room. "I'll be back in a minute," he called over his shoulder.

He came back a couple of minutes later and sat on the couch. "The only thing tougher than getting Miranda to bed is getting both Max and Miranda down for the count. I wonder what we're going to do when Cat has the baby?"

"Pray a lot," Jack said.

Mark laughed. "Good idea."

"How much longer until the baby's due?" Jack asked. He knew from seeing Cat that it couldn't be too much longer.

"Eight weeks. Since Miranda was early we're a little worried this one might be, too, but the doc says everything's looking good."

"Funny thing, I can remember Cynthia's last month with Cole, even fifteen years later." He shook his head. "It's uh, tough, to say the least."

"So tell me about this favor you want."

"Cole's birthday is a week from Sunday. I'm getting him a car, and I wondered if I could keep it in your garage overnight. I'll pick it up Saturday while he's at work."

"Sure, that shouldn't be a problem. I'll just park mine in the driveway for the night."

"Thanks, I really appreciate it. I hope it's not too much of a pain, but I want him to have it on his birthday."

"Hard to believe he's going to be sixteen. So tell me about this car. Is it new?"

Jack laughed. "No way. But at least it runs. He's been wanting one for months, but I've been ignoring him so I don't think he suspects anything."

"Mark, can you come here? Max wants you," Cat called from the other room.

"Be right there." He stood and said, "Want to hang around for a beer?"

"Thanks, but I'll pass. Cole's supposedly doing his homework, but I have a feeling he's playing video games. I'll let myself out."

"Sounds good. See you later," Mark said, and went to help his wife.

Jack pulled open the door and did a double take. "Ava? What are you doing here?"

She looked as surprised to see him as he was to see her. For a long moment she didn't speak. "I— This isn't your house, is it?"

"No. It's my—"

Before he could finish his sentence, Mark came back in saying, "I thought I heard—" He broke off as Jack stepped aside. He stood staring at Ava, rooted to the spot, the color completely drained from his face. After a long, tense moment, he said brokenly, "Miranda?"

Ava faltered, then stepped inside and said, "Yes, Mark. It's me. Miranda."

Jack didn't think either of them missed him when he walked out the door and closed it behind him.

FOR A LONG, INTENSE MOMENT they simply stared at each other. Then, Ava took a halting step forward and the next thing she knew, she was hugging her brother for the first time in over twenty years. Tears streamed down her cheeks. She couldn't have spoken if she'd tried.

When Mark finally loosened his hold, he wiped his eyes with the back of his hand and cleared his throat. Then he reached out hesitantly and touched her shoulder, as if he couldn't believe she was real. "My God, it's really you. How— Why—" He halted, searched her face. "I thought you were dead," he murmured. "We all did. It's been so long. We tried to find you for years. Years."

"I'm sorry," she whispered. "So sorry I didn't find you before now."

"Why didn't you? And why now?" His eyes narrowed. "You're the marine biologist Jack's been working with."

She nodded. "Yes. I go by Ava Vincent. I have for a long time." She looked around, noting the birdcage in the corner, covered for the night. "Your house is lovely. And you look so…so happy." She resisted the urge to wring her hands. He was still standing there, staring at her. "Could we—could we sit down?"

A small, dark haired pregnant woman entered the room, talking. "I finally got them to sleep. And I have to tell you I'm one step behind them. I'm so tired I could cry." She stopped abruptly when she caught sight of Ava. "Oh, I didn't realize we had company." Looking from Mark to Ava, her eyes widened, her hand went to her mouth. "Oh, my God," she whispered.

Mark cleared his throat again, held out a hand to his wife. She came immediately to his side. "This is Miranda. My sister."

To Miranda he said, "This is my wife, Cat."

Feeling incredibly awkward, Ava extended her hand. "It's wonderful to meet you." She gave a shaky laugh. "I don't quite know what to say."

Cat shook hands with her, looking nearly as dazed as Mark did. "I think I should leave you two alone. You'll have a lot to talk about." She turned to her husband. "Do you want me to call Jay?"

"No. I'd better do that."

Cat squeezed his hand and left the room.

"Jay's here, too, isn't he?" Ava said. "I saw him in the phone book." Mark nodded. "And Brian? Is he here? Is he all right?"

"He's fine. And no, he's not here. He's in China. I think. He works for an international company and travels all over the world." He motioned to the couch. "Have a seat. I'm going to call Jay." He started to walk out of the room but turned and looked at her. "Why did you wait so long?"

"It—it's a long story."

"I'll call Jay," he said. "And maybe then you can come up with a better answer." He left the room.

He's angry, she thought. And who could blame him? She was obviously hale and hearty. He said he had spent years looking for her. He deserved better from her. Mark had put himself between her and their father more times than she could count. He'd protected her, protected all of them, from their father's emotional abuse as much as he could, given that he'd been a child, too. But Mark hadn't been there that last night. No one had. And Ava had paid dearly. And then she'd run. Because she was a coward.

"Jay will be here in a few minutes," Mark said, walking back in. "He's a doctor now. He moved here from Los Angeles about a year and a half ago."

"I still see him as a seven-year-old. It's hard for me to wrap my mind around that."

"It's hard for me to wrap my mind around the fact that you're here, in Aransas City. And that I don't even know what to call you."

"Call me Ava. I've been her for a lot longer than I was Miranda Kincaid."

He studied her a moment before he spoke. "Did you know I was here?"

"No. Not until I saw your picture in the local paper. I wondered— I thought you might still be in Texas, but I didn't know you'd moved here, to Aransas City."

"And I'm betting you wouldn't have taken that job if you'd known it," he said drily. "Would you have, Miranda— Damn it, Ava, or whoever you are."

"It wasn't you, Mark. It was never you."

"I know who to blame," he said bitterly. "Our father. But hating that bastard doesn't explain why you never tried to find me or Jay or Brian. Or Mom. Unless you hated all of us, too."

Evading the topic of their mother, she said, "I don't hate you and Jay and Brian. Of course I don't. How could you think that?"

"It's easy, since you never tried to find us. I used to wonder what it would feel like to see you again. I thought I'd be so happy to see you that I wouldn't care why you'd run or why you never tried to find us. But I do care." His hand curled into a fist. "It hurts, more than I'd ever imagined. Why didn't you trust me?"

"I'm sorry," she whispered. "So sorry." And the story she told him wouldn't satisfy him, she knew.

"He walked out a year or two after you left. Nobody's seen him since."

Ava closed her eyes. If only she'd known that. But by then it had been too late. She'd already taken that irreversible step.

"You haven't asked about Mom."

"No," she said in a low voice. "I haven't. And

I won't." She didn't want to know about the woman who'd let her down so badly.

"It wasn't her fault," Mark said. "She was sick."

Ava held up a hand. "Please, do we have to get into this now?"

"We have to sometime. Now seems appropriate to me." The doorbell rang and Mark went to answer it. She stood up, nervously biting her lip and wondering if Jay would be as angry and conflicted as Mark appeared to be about their reunion. Maybe he wouldn't care one way or the other. After all, he'd been so young when she'd left he probably barely remembered her.

She heard them talking, their voices low. Then Mark swung the door wide and a tall, blond, very handsome man stepped inside. He didn't hesitate but came right to her. "So, do you have a hug for your little brother?" he asked, flashing her the same grin he'd had at seven.

He hugged her and the tears that had threatened the whole time she was talking to Mark spilled down her cheeks. "You're a man," she sobbed. "I can't believe you're so old."

He just laughed and patted her back.

CHAPTER SIX

AVA COULDN'T STOP CRYING. The harder she tried, the faster the tears ran down her cheeks. Finally Mark brought her a box of tissues. As he gave it to her, she thought she felt him smooth a hand over her hair, but she couldn't be sure. And, as angry and hurt as he seemed, she doubted he had. Why should he have? She didn't deserve tenderness after what she'd put him through. Pulling a tissue out, she blew her nose, then dabbed at her eyes and cheeks and drew in a deep breath, slowly gaining control.

Tremulously, she smiled at Jay, then sat on the couch before her legs gave way. "I don't usually cry. Not like that."

"You're allowed," he said, clearing his throat. "I'm a little…emotional, too. So's Mark."

Ava risked another glance at Mark. Emotional? Maybe but anger looked like the primary emotion he was battling.

Jay and Mark both sat down. Ava noticed Mark chose the chair rather than sit beside her.

Ava wadded up the tissue and looked down at her hands. "I'm not sure where to start."

"At the beginning," Mark said. "Tell us what happened the night you ran away."

She drew in another deep breath. "All right." She closed her eyes, gearing up to tell a story she'd told to only two people. Jim and Jeri Vincent, the people who'd taken her in all those years ago. The doctor who had saved her life and his wife, who'd loved her from the first. The Vincents, the parents of her heart, had passed away three years earlier, within a couple of months of each other. She still missed them and knew she always would.

"I was home alone. I don't know where everyone else was. I think you'd taken the boys somewhere, Mark. Overnight. And Mother—" She broke off and gave a bitter laugh. "I'm sure she was doing something for one of her causes.

"Father came home and told me to fix him something to eat. I made him a sandwich. A turkey sandwich with Swiss cheese. I still remember that and haven't been able to eat one since. I can't even look at one without getting nauseous."

She looked at Mark. "You know how he was. He didn't like the way I made it. He started berating me, calling me useless, cursing at me. He threw the sandwich on the floor. The floor I'd just finished mopping, so he wouldn't be mad when he came home and found it dirty. Because Mother, of course, was too busy to do it." She stopped, shook it off. None of that mattered now. "He told me to clean it up because I was so stupid that's all I was good for." She put her fist to her mouth, not wanting to go on.

Jay reached out and squeezed her other hand. "Easy," he said. "Did you do it?"

She shook her head and dropped her eyes, looking down at their joined hands. "I told him to do it himself."

"Shit." The single word Mark said conveyed a wealth of understanding.

She raised her eyes to meet his and nodded. "Yes, not a bright thing for me to do. He backhanded me across the mouth. I was…shocked by how quickly it happened." And by how much it had hurt.

Mark looked ill, which only made her feel that much worse. "I didn't think he'd hit you," he said. "He'd hit me a few times, but his thing always seemed to be more mental than physical."

"Usually it was. I think he enjoyed making us feel like nothing, less than nothing. He got off on the mind games. But that night was the first time he actually hit me. I don't know—" She shrugged, remembering the helpless horror when she realized what she'd done. "My defiance made him crazy. It must have broken some control he'd been keeping. I was bleeding and crying, but he made me get down on my hands and knees and scrub up the mess and the blood. Then he locked me in my room and told me I'd be sorry I'd disrespected him like I had. He would make me pay for it."

"So you ran away."

Jay looked as sick as Mark did. "Yes, I was afraid he'd hurt me again. I'd never seen him quite like that. So angry, so…crazy." She shook her head, battling the memories. "That wasn't the end of it. Not yet. It gets worse. Much worse."

"I should never have left you alone with him," Mark said. "Damn it, I knew what he was like. I should have known—"

She reached out for him, then let her hand drop. He wasn't ready to accept comfort from her. "It's not your fault, Mark. You couldn't have known. You were sixteen, you were a child. Just as I was."

He shook his head, clasped his hands together, arms on his thighs and leaned forward. "Tell us the rest."

"I went out the window. I'm sure he didn't imagine I'd dare disobey him again. I didn't know where else to go, so I went to Brad's house. My boyfriend," she added for Jay's benefit. Brad Sanderson had been her first boyfriend. A lifetime ago.

"His parents were gone. He didn't know what to do for me. I was…pretty hysterical. Not making much sense, I'm sure. Finally, he calmed me down, promised we'd get help. I wanted to believe him, desperately, even though I was afraid to. But he was so sweet, so comforting, and I think he really did care about me." She fell silent, not anxious to finish the story. But she felt Mark's gaze on her and forced herself to continue.

"If I'd stopped to think, I would never have gone to Brad. I'm sure it was the first place Father looked when he realized I'd gone. We'd left the front door unlocked. He kicked open the door of Brad's bedroom and…found us together."

Caught in the act. It had been the first time for both of them. Neither of them had meant for it to happen. But she'd been so upset, and Brad had been so sweet. And her father had turned what should have been a precious memory into something horrible. Something she couldn't remember without feeling the pain of what came afterward.

"He didn't kill him," Mark said. "We'd have known if he had. He'd have gone to jail."

"No," she said, thankful she hadn't had to spell out exactly what had happened for her brothers. "He said some awful things to Brad, but he saved the brunt of his anger for me. He dragged me out of there, promising me I'd be sorry. Brad was too scared to come after us. I couldn't blame him."

"It didn't occur to him to call the cops?" Jay asked.

"Why would it? What would he have told the police? He was my father, I'm sure Brad thought there was nothing he could do." Her tears had dried and she didn't mean to start again. If she allowed herself to cry now, she'd never get through the remainder of the story.

"Go on," Mark said harshly. "I want to know what the bastard did to you when he got you home."

"I'm sure you've guessed. No one was home. He had all the time in the world to do whatever he wanted." Her gaze met Mark's and held. "He beat me." And cursed her. She could still hear his voice, shouting at her. *Whore,* he'd called her. And worse.

"He didn't touch my face, not after that first time, earlier in the kitchen. He used his fists and when that didn't satisfy him, he took a belt to me. He whipped me with that until I bled, until I wanted to die. I'd have done anything to stop it, but I couldn't make him quit. The more I begged, the harder I cried, the more he whipped me."

She couldn't stop the shudder that coursed through her as the terrible memories swamped her. "I thought he was going to kill me. Then he kicked me and I passed out. I think he broke my rib. When I woke up, I was lying on the floor of my bedroom. I was afraid he had killed me. Except I hurt too much, so I knew I had to be alive."

"God!" The word burst from Mark. He took her hand and said fiercely, "Why didn't you come to me? I'd have killed the bastard."

"I know you would have." She'd been terrified he would, if he'd walked in. "That wasn't all. He said if I told anyone what he'd done, he would—" She broke off, pulled her hand from Mark's and curved her arm over her stomach, protecting what couldn't be protected. "He said he'd take a belt to the boys and beat them black and blue. Like he had me but worse. He'd make me watch while he beat them, and it would be my fault." Yet even knowing that, even knowing what she might be exposing her brothers to, she'd run.

"He'd have had to go through me first," Mark said.

"He knew that. And he would have. No, don't shake your head at me, Mark. He'd have done it. He said he'd take care of you first. You know he always hated you for sticking up for us, for me and the boys. He'd have killed you and been happy doing it."

"He was a chickenshit, Miranda. He couldn't have taken me on, not by the time I was sixteen."

Her father's words rang in her ears. Words of malice and hatred. Words of evil. *I'll do Mark first. That little bastard will pay for all the lip he's given me.*

"He never touched us," Jay added. "Like Mark said, it was always the mental. Maybe after what he did to you he was afraid to."

The relief she felt was monumental. At least he hadn't hurt the boys—physically, anyway. The guilt of knowing their father might have beaten them anyway had been with her for years. But it hadn't been enough to make her go back.

"I couldn't be sure what he'd do. I only knew I couldn't face another beating, because he'd have killed me the next time. So, I waited until he left the house and I took every dime I could find. I knew where Mother kept a stash. I'm sure it was charity money, but at that point I didn't care. I took it, along with what jewelry she had that I could find, and I left."

"How did you do it with the injuries you had?"

She shrugged, wearily. "I had no choice. I tore up a pillowcase and wrapped it around my ribs. It helped…some. Then I hitchhiked to the bus station and left town on the first bus headed out of state."

"The police traced you that far," Mark murmured. "To the bus station. You bought a ticket to Memphis. But then you vanished."

She hadn't made it to Memphis, she remembered. She'd got off the stop before that and bought another ticket, still headed east. Her money had finally run out close to the Florida-Alabama border. She'd been stranded in a small town she didn't even know the name of with ten dollars in her pocket. She'd hitchhiked the rest of the way into Florida, to Pensacola. Some college kids had given her a lift. They were the last good thing she remembered until the Vincents had taken her in three months later.

"I remember him freaking out the next day, when we found out you were gone," Jay said. "Brian and I hid. We didn't know what he was going to do."

"Mom called the cops," Mark said. "He didn't want her to, but for once she overrode him."

"He really never hit you? None of you?" Ava asked. Both Mark and Jay shook their heads. "I guess my leaving did something good then."

"I can understand why you ran away," Mark said. "I never questioned that you'd had a good reason for leaving. But you never tried to get in touch with us. Not once, in more than twenty years."

"I—I was afraid."

"After five years? Or ten years? Or fifteen? Were you still afraid then?"

More so than she could ever tell him. But not of her father. She was afraid they would turn from her once they heard the rest.

"Let me get you some water," Jay said. "You look like you could use it, and I know I could."

Jay left the room and she looked at Mark. "I'm sorry."

"Yeah, you said that." He shoved a hand through his hair. "I know you were young, and scared. But I don't understand how you could go all that time letting us think you were dead. I thought you were dead," he repeated. "Because I couldn't imagine you were alive and had never tried to find us in all those years."

It broke her heart to hear him talk that way. But there was nothing she could say.

"Mark." Jay had come back in and handed her a glass of water. He gave one to Mark and kept the other for himself. "Let her finish. It's obviously not easy for her."

"It's not easy for any of us. Not for you either, even though you're acting like it is."

Jay put his hand on his brother's shoulder. "It's okay, Mark. She's here now. That's the important thing."

Mark didn't look too sure of that but he said nothing else. Ava sipped the water then began again. "I headed east. I'm not sure how long it took me. Days. A week. Longer. Anyway, I wound up in Pensacola, Florida. By then I had no money, no idea what I was going to do. Someone had stolen my backpack and all I had was what was in my pockets." She spread her hands. "Which was damn little at that point."

"What did you do?" Jay asked. "I have to tell you that as the father of young girls I don't like to think about what that must have been like for you."

"You have children?"

He smiled for the first time since she'd begun her story. "Three. Roxy and Mel, who are twelve and ten. And a son, Jason, who's a little over a year old."

"Twelve and ten? You must have been—" She broke off, realizing she'd been about to put her foot in her mouth.

Jay laughed. "Relax, I didn't start that young. The girls are my stepdaughters." He glanced at his brother, who sat silent. "Mark has two kids with another on the way. Max is five. Miranda's two years old."

Ava stared at Mark. "You named your daughter after me?" she finally managed to whisper.

Mark's eyes, blue and tortured, met hers. "Yeah. We named her after my sister. The one we thought was dead."

There had been times when she'd wanted to

die. Wished she could. Had even thought about ending it, but she hadn't. "Would you rather I were dead?" He made an impatient gesture, which she took to be negative. "We don't have to do this. I can leave and not come back. If we see each other, we can pretend we don't even know each other. Is that what you want?"

"No." He said it quietly, but she heard the suppressed emotion behind the word. "I don't know what I want. But I know I deserve an explanation."

"Please try to understand." But he wouldn't. Because she couldn't tell him the real reason she'd dropped out of their lives so completely.

"For a little more than three months I lived…on the streets." Technically not the truth, but close enough. "I'm not going to talk about it. Once I got out I swore I wouldn't talk about it or think about it. Ever. It's the only way I was able to go on. So if that bothers you, if you think you have to know, then you'll just have to either get over it or forget about me."

"How did you get off the streets? Did social services find you?" Jay asked.

"No, thank God, or they'd have sent me back home. A wonderful couple took me in. Jim and

Jeri Vincent. He was a doctor. If it hadn't been for them I'd have died."

"They adopted you? How?" Mark asked.

"Not legally. Informally. I never told them my name. I was too afraid of having to go back. To him. So I became Ava Vincent."

"Didn't they ever try to find out who you really were?"

"Yes, several times. After a while they quit. They realized I would never go back to my parents. That I'd rather die than go back. So they left me alone, loved me, and gave me a chance at another life."

They had stopped asking about her parents when she'd threatened to go back on the streets. To go back to the life she'd been living before Jim took care of her in the E.R. and saved her life. They'd freed her from that life, the one she'd accepted as the only way to survive. Her life as a teenage prostitute with nowhere to go but down.

CHAPTER SEVEN

"YOU LOOK EXHAUSTED," Jay said. "We don't have to talk about everything tonight. Maybe you should go home, get some sleep. We can talk again later. Tomorrow, or this weekend even."

She was beyond exhausted, she was an emotional wreck. Even so, there was one more thing she needed to know. "All right. But before I go could you tell me more about Brian? How he is and what he's doing? Mark said he works for an international company."

Jay smiled. "Yeah, he's a computer geek. We're not sure exactly what he does with them. It involves industrial espionage, I think." He checked his watch. "I can try to call him. It's morning in China."

"Will he want to talk to me?" Brian had been even younger than Jay when she'd left. He probably didn't remember her at all. In fact, she wasn't sure Jay really remembered her, even though he acted as if he did.

"I'll call him," Mark said, and left the room abruptly.

She looked after him wistfully before turning to Jay. "He hates me, doesn't he?"

"Of course he doesn't hate you. But—" He rubbed a hand over his brow. "He's hurt. You have to remember, Mark knew you better than either Brian or I did. I think he's always felt responsible that you left and that he couldn't find you. Mark's a very responsible guy. He's had to be. You wouldn't know this, but he raised Brian and me on his own from the time we were twelve and eleven."

Unwillingly, she asked, "Why? What happened to Mother? You said she's alive."

"Yes. She's fine now, but back then she was sick. She spent two years in a hospital, being treated for depression. She didn't tell us, though, she just left us with Mark. He was all of twenty-one. Mom didn't contact us for years after that because she thought we'd hate her for dumping us on Mark like she did."

It didn't sit well that she had deserting her family in common with her mother. Ava didn't want to have anything in common with the woman who'd given birth to her. "Did you hate her? Do you hate her?"

He shook his head. "No. Brian and I never did. Especially not once we found out why she'd left us. We reconciled several years ago. Mark had a harder time with forgiving her than Brian and I did. So she and Mark took a little longer to work things out. But they did." He paused and added, "Mom looked for you, too, Miranda. She had a private detective looking for you almost from the day you disappeared."

"Too little too late," Ava said. "I don't want to talk about her."

Jay hesitated. "We have to tell her you're alive."

"No."

"I'm telling her. I'm sorry if that upsets you, but I'm not keeping the fact that you're alive from our mother."

He looked implacable and she suspected he was. "I can't stop you from telling her, but I won't see her."

"That's your decision, but I hope you'll reconsider."

When pigs flew. Maybe she was wrong to

blame her mother for so much, but the bottom line remained. Her mother had put up with her husband's abuse and left her children to deal with it as well. If she'd only left the son of a bitch…Ava might never have been forced to run away. And if she hadn't run away she would never have become a prostitute. If she'd never been a prostitute, she'd never have gotten pregnant. She wouldn't have a past so shameful she couldn't share it with anyone.

Her past had ruined her marriage for a number of reasons, not the least of which was she'd never been able to be honest with her husband. She'd told him very little about her past. Oh, she'd told him she couldn't have children, but she'd lied about the reason why. And she'd lied about why she refused to adopt. She couldn't tell him or anyone why she didn't deserve to adopt a child.

If she shared the truth with her brothers, it would kill any hope of knowing them again, of becoming a part of their lives. She couldn't share her past with them; she couldn't share it with anyone.

But Jay was talking about the present. And their mother. "I'm sorry, I won't see her. I can't."

Jay didn't say anything but she didn't believe that was the end of the subject. At least for now he was dropping it.

"Can I ask you something?" she said after a moment.

"Sure."

"Do you remember me? You were so young…"

"Not so young that I could forget you. You used to read to me and Brian. I remember we'd get on either side of you on the couch and you'd read for hours. We loved it." He stopped and smiled at her, that easy smile that caused a pang for all the years she'd missed. "We loved you. We still love you, Miranda. Mark does too, he's just having a hard time understanding."

"What about you?"

He rubbed his chin, looking at her thoughtfully. "To be honest, I don't understand either. But I can wait until you feel like talking."

"What if I never do?"

"I guess we'll cross that bridge when we come to it. Maybe…maybe it doesn't matter why you found us again. Only that you have."

Mark came back into the room. "I tried all his numbers and couldn't reach him. I left a message for him to call me. I told him it was urgent but not to worry. Why don't you leave me your phone numbers and I'll give them to him when he calls."

He handed her a pad and she wrote her numbers on it, then made another copy for Jay, tore off the sheet and handed it to him. "I'm not sure when I'll have a home number. I bought a house and I'm supposed to move in Friday, but who knows when I'll get local service. I've written down my office and cell numbers, though." Feeling awkward, she stood. "I'd better get going. I have to be in the office early tomorrow and I'm staying in Port Aransas until I can get moved in."

Jay stood as well. "Mark, what about Sunday? You know, the barbecue."

Mark looked at him blankly for a moment, then shrugged. Turning to her he said, "Cat and I are having a barbecue Sunday afternoon. Why don't you come?"

She didn't believe he really wanted her there. If Jay hadn't prodded him he wouldn't have asked her. But she couldn't resist. "I'd love to. Thank you."

They both walked her to the door. Jay hugged her easily, then released her. Unsure whether to make the first move, she looked at Mark, who was frowning at her.

"Oh, hell," he said, and reached for her. He held her close for a moment then let go.

She hoped she could make it to her car before she broke down and cried.

"YOU WERE A LITTLE HARD on her, weren't you?" Jay said to Mark as soon as the door shut behind Miranda.

No, damn it, not Miranda. *Ava.* "No more than she deserved."

"That's not fair."

Mark looked at his brother. "I'll tell you what's not fair. It's pretty unfair that she waited more than twenty years to finally look us up. And she wouldn't have done it if she hadn't been forced into it. She as much as admitted that to me before you came over."

"You don't know that. And we don't know what her reasons were for not getting in touch."

"No, and it doesn't sound like she's in any hurry to tell us, does it?"

"Give her time," he repeated. "I know you're hurting."

"And you're not?"

Jay put his hand on Mark's shoulder and squeezed. "Not as much as you are."

Mark looked away. Finally he said, "I had to tell myself she was dead. I couldn't stand it any longer, looking for her and never finding her. Damn it, she vanished without a trace. What else could I think? And then to have her show up here. Out of the blue…I was so happy to see her I could have cried."

"Mark, I think she will talk to you, but you have to give her some time."

"I don't have much choice, do I?"

"There's always a choice." He paused and added, "You forgave Mom for leaving us. Don't you think you could do the same for Miranda?"

"It's not the same. I never blamed Miranda for leaving. Even when I didn't know exactly what the bastard had done to her, I didn't blame her. Do you think I'd blame her now?"

"No. But maybe she has just as compelling a reason for not trying to find us as she did for leaving in the first place."

"Maybe. I guess we'll see." Or they wouldn't. "We have to tell Mom."

"Yes. Ava doesn't want us to. I told her that wasn't an option. She refuses to see her, though."

"Great. I get to tell Mom we've found Miranda but she doesn't want to see her. It's going to kill her."

"Do you want me to do it?"

He'd gladly let Jay do it, but that wouldn't be right. "No, it's my responsibility."

Jay smiled at him. "Everything isn't your responsibility, Mark. We're all grown now."

"Yeah, I know. But I think Mom will take the news better from me."

"All right. I sure as hell don't envy you that task." He glanced at his watch. "I'd better get home. Gail has no idea what's going on and I'll have to fill her in."

"Okay. See you Sunday." He'd see Miranda—Ava—Sunday, too. He hoped he could come to some sort of peace before that.

Mark locked up and checked on the kids. He kissed Max's cheek, stroked a hand over his dark hair, wondering how his son could look so angelic in sleep when he was such a pistol when he was awake. He went to Miranda's room next, adjusted her covers and kissed her soft baby cheek. Miranda, the child they'd named after his dead sister. Except his sister was alive and well and calling herself Ava Vincent.

He stopped with his hand on his bedroom door. This late in her pregnancy Cat slept as much as possible. He knew how tired she was taking care of two jobs, two young kids and another on the way. But damn, if he'd ever needed to talk to his wife, it was now. He turned the knob and stepped inside.

She was reading, or pretending to read. Love swamped him as he looked at her, this woman who had changed his life. Who had given him love and children he loved more than he could ever have imagined. The woman who had even helped him reconcile with his mother. The woman he'd always considered his own personal miracle.

Her smile bloomed when she saw him. She set the book down and said nothing but simply held out her arms. It wasn't the first time he'd realized how blessed he was to have a wife who not only loved him but understood him.

He gathered her in his arms and held on tightly, wishing he knew what to do with the mix of emotions he'd experienced since walking into the den and seeing Miranda.

"Do you want to talk about it?" she asked.

"I'd rather just hold you. And have you hold me."

"Then that's what we'll do," she said, and pulled his face down to kiss him.

CHAPTER EIGHT

JACK TOOK THE TRASH OUT to the curb, still thinking about Ava and Mark and the whole unbelievable scene he'd witnessed. And the one he hadn't. Obviously, his suspicions, wild as they'd seemed, had been right on the money.

Ava really was Miranda Kincaid, the sister Mark had believed was dead. He wondered why she'd disappeared for so many years and why she'd finally decided to find her brothers. Or had she meant to find them? Maybe it had been a coincidence. If so, what a shock to the system that would have been. For all of them.

He set the trash bags down and glanced at Mark's house. Ava's car was still parked at the curb but even as he looked, he saw the taillights come on and she drove off slowly. A short way down the street, she pulled over and stopped.

Torn between wanting to make sure she was all

right and not wanting to butt in to what was clearly none of his business, he hesitated. "Oh, hell," he muttered, and walked down the street to her car.

The streetlamp gave off enough light that he could see inside, though not too clearly. Sure enough, her head was down on the steering wheel and he thought her shoulders were shaking. He rapped on the window.

Her head jerked up and she stared at him. He made a motion for her to roll down the window. She waited so long he didn't think she would do it, but she finally did. She didn't speak, just gazed at him with tear tracks on her cheeks. And she didn't look particularly happy to see him.

"Are you okay?"

She laughed, sounding anything but amused. "Yeah. Just wonderful."

"Can I do anything?"

"No. I can't talk. I need to leave."

He hesitated again. She was a grown woman. She could take care of herself. Why this compulsion to help her when she clearly didn't want a near stranger in her face? He ought to leave her alone but he knew he wouldn't. Instead, he walked around her car, opened the passenger-side door and slid inside.

"What do you think you're doing?" she asked, looking at him like he was a crazy man.

Making sure she didn't drive off, that's what. "Take a minute. You shouldn't drive when you're so upset."

Her hands tightened on the steering wheel. "What I do is none of your business. I'm perfectly capable of driving. I'm not going to have a wreck just because I'm upset."

"Trust me. It happens." He'd come to terms with his wife's death a long time ago. Or believed he had. But he still felt the swift surge of guilt whenever he remembered Cynthia's accident.

Her eyes widened as she stared at him. "Oh, God. Your wife. You said she died in an accident. A car accident…" Her voice trailed off and she looked sick.

He nodded and shrugged, pretending an acceptance of fate he didn't feel. "Like I said, it happens."

He recognized Jay's car as he pulled up beside them, stopped and rolled down his window. "Are you all right?" he called.

"I'm fine. Jack and I are just talking."

Jay didn't look too sure of that but he seemed to accept it. "Okay. You'll be at Mark's Sunday, right?"

"Mark only asked me because you twisted his arm."

"That's not true. He wants you there, and so do I. Promise me you'll come."

She hesitated a long moment, then said, "All right. I'll come."

Jay drove off and Ava turned back to Jack. "At least he doesn't seem to hate me."

"Mark doesn't hate you." If he knew his old friend at all, he knew that.

She didn't say anything and when she finally spoke she went back to the previous subject. "Your wife. The accident. Why…why was she upset?"

He sighed and rubbed a hand over the back of his neck. "You ever been married?"

"Yes. I'm divorced."

"Then you know how it works. We didn't fight a lot, but when we did—" He shook his head. "You know how sometimes you fight about stupid things? Things that really don't matter but you have a big knock-down, drag-out fight anyway?"

She smiled faintly. "I remember."

"It was about wallpaper. We fought for weeks over the damn wallpaper in the kitchen. Cynthia tried everything she could think of to get me to go for new wallpaper but I wouldn't. The more she pushed the more stubborn I was about it. No how, no way were we getting new wallpaper."

"Why? Couldn't you afford it?"

"Yeah. If we did the work. But I ran a charter fishing service then, and the last thing I wanted to do in my time off was wallpaper the kitchen. One Saturday, my first day off in weeks, we got into it again. Cynthia finally got fed up and said she was going to do it herself. Then she took off for the store. She left Cole at home with me." Usually, she took him with her. But that day he'd had a cold. It terrified him to think how close he'd come to losing both his wife and child. "It was raining. A nasty, messy day."

"That's when she had the accident."

He nodded. "She ran a stop sign. An eighteen-wheeler broadsided her, and that was it. They said…the doctors believed she died on impact, so at least she didn't suffer."

"I'm so sorry, Jack."

"Yeah." He looked at her. "If I'd known what was going to happen, I'd have wallpapered the whole goddamn house. It was such a stupid, stupid thing to fight about."

"You blame yourself for her accident, don't you?"

"Sometimes. Yeah, sometimes I do." He looked off in the distance before turning back to her. "I went to counseling. I know the guilt trip is not productive. I know she wouldn't want me to blame myself. But I still wonder if we hadn't been fighting would she have paid more attention?" He spread his hands. "Fruitless, but I can't seem to help it."

Hesitantly, she reached out and put her hand over his. "You shouldn't blame yourself. She shares the burden. Unlike—" She broke off and withdrew her hand.

"Unlike?" he prompted.

Her mouth tightened into a thin line. "Unlike me, I was going to say. Mark hates me, and he has every reason to. None of this is his fault."

Maybe there'd been a point to him sharing that story. She'd needed to hear it so she could talk about her own. "I'm sure Mark doesn't hate you," he said again. She remained silent. "I take it the reunion didn't go well."

She laughed harshly. "You could say that." Then she glanced at him speculatively. "How did you know it was a reunion?"

"It wasn't that hard to figure out, especially given your resemblance to each other. And right before I left you admitted you were Miranda."

She shrugged, then said haltingly, "At first Mark was happy to see me. I know he was. But later, after he'd had time to think it over—" She broke off, pressing her fingers to her temples. "He hates me."

"I've known Mark a long time. Sixteen, no seventeen years now. And until the other day I never knew he had a sister. But it wasn't because he'd forgotten you. I think it hurt him too much to talk about it. When he told me about his lost sister, the one he thought had died, he sure didn't sound like he hated you."

"Not then, not when he didn't know I was all right. You don't understand. I vanished without a trace, and I never contacted him. Never contacted any of my brothers. Not once in all those years."

"Why didn't you?"

"I couldn't. I wanted to…but I just couldn't."

"Did you tell him why?"

"No," she said, her voice low. "I couldn't do that either. And he doesn't understand."

That made two of them, but if she wouldn't tell her brothers she obviously wouldn't tell him. "Why would he ask you to come to his house again if he hated you?"

"Because Jay made him. Jay isn't as angry at

me as Mark is. I'm not sure why. Maybe because
he was so young when I left. Or maybe…maybe
it didn't hurt him as much as it did Mark. After
all, he hardly knew me."

"Are you ever going to tell them why you lost
touch?"

"Not if I can possibly help it." She looked at
him. "You think I'm awful, too, don't you?"

"Look, Ava, I don't know enough about what's
going on or what went on to know what to think."
He shoved a hand through his hair, still finding it
hard to believe. "But you obviously care about
your brothers and what they think, or you
wouldn't be this upset."

"Just answer the question. Do you think I'm
horrible for not telling them why I never tried to
find them?"

His gaze locked with hers. "I think you must
have a damn good reason. And I also think you're
going to have a tough time reconciling totally with
any of them, especially Mark, unless you do tell
them."

"I think so, too." She sighed and added,
"Which means I'm screwed."

Jack laughed. "I said tough, not impossible."

"Semantics," she said. After a moment she

spoke again. "Why are you being so nice to me? You hardly know me. And you said yourself you're an old friend of Mark's. It seems like you'd be on his side in all this."

"No one told me I had to choose sides." She said nothing, just continued to look at him. He patted her hand, which lay on the seat between them. "You looked like you could use a friend. I thought I'd offer."

"That's it? You didn't have another reason?"

Man, she was suspicious. He'd felt her stiffen when he touched her hand. "Like what?"

Her eyes narrowed. "I don't know. Maybe you have an ulterior motive."

"Oh, sure. Like what?" he repeated.

"You tell me."

"What, you think I'm being nice so I can maneuver you into bed?"

"I didn't say that."

"But you thought it."

"All right. Yes, it crossed my mind."

He couldn't deny he'd thought about taking her to bed. Not that he'd had any intention of following up on the idea. And for sure he didn't plan on maneuvering her into something she didn't want to do. But she was beautiful and single and he was single and lonely, and hell, he was just a man. Who wouldn't think about it? Which, of course, really burned him. He hated to be so predictable.

"That's some ego you've got there, lady."

She'd been glaring at him but at that her gaze fell.

"You're right. I'm...sorry. But you did ask me to dinner. So I wondered—" She fumbled for words, then swore. "Damn it, now I feel like a fool. It's just men, most men— Oh, forget it. I'm sorry if I insulted you."

He tilted his head, considering her. "Does every man who asks you out try to get you into bed?"

She snorted. "Most of them."

"But you were tempted to go out with me when I asked you. Weren't you?"

She pursed her lips, answering reluctantly. "Yes. I thought you were nice. I enjoyed talking to you on the boat. You didn't make innuendos, or...comments, like so many men do. And it didn't really sound like a date, at the time. More like just grabbing a bite after work, which is entirely different."

"You have a very suspicious nature, you know that?"

"With good reason."

"I haven't even kissed you. I haven't even made a move like I want to kiss you."

"I know. I said I was sorry. I'm upset and I jumped to conclusions. I have a habit of doing that where men are concerned."

"Do you automatically condemn a man just because the poor slob tries to kiss you? Or wants to kiss you?"

"No, of course I don't. I—" She glared at him. "I have no idea how we got onto this subject. This is ridiculous."

"Maybe so, but you're not crying anymore."

Her lips curved into a smile. "You're right, I'm not."

"So my job is done." He got out and leaned down to look at her through the open door. "Drive carefully, Ava."

"Jack," she called as he walked away. He stopped and turned back to her. "Thanks."

"No problemo." No, the problem was, now instead of a low-grade urge, he wanted to kiss her so badly he could taste it. God, he wanted to taste her. And somehow he didn't think that was going to happen any time soon.

CHAPTER NINE

AVA DIDN'T SEE JACK the next day. Just as well, she thought. After all, she'd basically made a fool of herself by jumping to the conclusion that he was coming on to her. Maybe if she hadn't been so rattled from seeing her brothers, she wouldn't have. She'd never know now.

He'd been very kind. Maybe his object really had been to take her mind off her troubles. The tactic had certainly worked, she had to admit.

She and Jack weren't due to go out on the bay again until the following week, since she was taking Friday off to move. So that gave her a little time to think how she would approach Jack the next time she saw him. Right now ignoring the whole situation sounded good to her.

She pulled the memory chip from her camera and downloaded the images onto her computer. These would go in the central database, to be matched against the ones already entered. If the picture didn't match with one of those, she would have to sort through the analog images, and none of them were online. Book after book of them, many of which were in their library. She meant to do what she could to put them into the online database but it was a long, tedious process. Still, having to sort through books and match pictures manually made her work take longer, as well.

Someone knocked on her door. "Come in."

"Dr. Vincent?"

A young man of about fifteen or sixteen stood in her doorway. She knew he was Jack's son the minute she saw him. He had the same hair color, though he wore it longer. The shape of his face was similar to Jack's as well, though his eyes were whisky-brown, rather than the brilliant green of his father's.

"Yes, can I help you?"

"I'm Cole Williams. Dr. Long said I should ask you if there's anything you need me to do. I work here after school," he added unnecessarily.

She hid a smile at his manner. Trying hard to be offhand, but she could see the eagerness and curiosity peeking through. "Dr. Long doesn't have something else in mind for you?"

Cole shrugged. "He said I could help with the dolphin tank, but right now there aren't any dolphins needing to be rehabbed. So he sent me to some of the other offices to see if anyone else needs help."

She started to say she didn't need any, but it dawned on her there was a job he might be well suited for. And one that could help her out a lot. "How are you with computers?"

"Pretty good."

"How would you like to help me convert analog images of dolphin dorsal fins to digital and transfer them to an online database?"

"Sure. You want me to use that computer?" he asked, pointing to her new pride and joy.

"No, that baby is mine," she said with a laugh. "I'm going to set you up on my laptop in the library. That's where the images are. It's tedious work, but it's important to my project."

"That's okay. I don't mind. I'd rather do something on the computer than some of the stuff they've had me doing."

She got up to lead the way to the library. "What else have you been doing?"

"Helping the janitor." He made a face at that. "And helping my dad clean his boat. He's the research fleet captain."

"Yes, we've met. He took me out on the bay yesterday." And consoled her last night. "I'm doing a study of dorsal fin identification of dolphins in the Aransas Bay area."

"Cool. So you're a marine biologist?"

"Yes. A marine mammalogist to be exact. Are you interested in dolphins, Cole?" She opened the library door and motioned for him to go in.

"Yes, ma'am. They rock." He looked around the library at the shelves full of notebooks. "Do all these have to be inputted?" He sounded apprehensive.

Ava laughed. "No, some are already in the database. Don't feel you have to do it all. There's enough to keep three people busy for a year. I just want to make a start. We'll go from the most recent," she said, pulling down a notebook. "About four years ago everyone began to switch to digital. These are from the years prior to that."

"Is it hard to do?"

"Not really. Just time consuming. Dr. Long said he hoped we'd have a new computer for this, but in the meantime we'll use my laptop."

She accessed the data bank, shrank it, then showed him the program to convert the files. "Then once you've converted a file, you can scan it in and add it to the database."

"Like this?" He went through the process, impressing her with how easy it had been for him.

"Just like that," she said, happy that he caught on so quickly. "Are you sure you haven't done anything like this before?"

"It's a little like one of my computer games."

"Really? Well, who'd have thought that. Let me know if you run into any problems, okay?"

"Okay, thanks." He flashed her a smile that was remarkably like his father's and went back to the computer, apparently eager to get to work.

"How are you at photography?" she asked.

He looked up and smiled again. "I have a camera."

Ava laughed. "I just wondered if you might like to go out with your dad and me sometime to take pictures of the dolphin. One weekend, perhaps."

He lit up like a neon sign. "That would be awesome. Are you sure you don't mind?"

"Not a bit. I could use the help."

"Dr. Long only pays me for after-school hours."

"I have a feeling the budget might stretch to include an occasional weekend. Especially since if any dolphins come in you'll be working weekends anyway. We'll see what we can do," she told him and left him to it.

Nice kid, she thought. She wondered if he and his father got along. That was sure something outside her experience. She thought about Mark's barbecue on Sunday, wondering if Jack and his son would be there. She hoped they would be. She could use all the friendly faces she could get.

"MARK, WHAT ARE YOU DOING?" Cat asked him Sunday after lunch. "Don't you know what time it is? People are going to start getting here soon." She glanced at her watch. "Well, a couple of hours, anyway."

Since he was sitting on the side of the bed doing dumbbell curls, he took that for a rhetorical question and grunted without answering.

She propped her hands on her hips, tapped her foot and narrowed her eyes at him. "What's wrong?"

"Nothing. Why?" He did two more curls and forced himself to rest.

"Gee, I don't know. You wouldn't go to church with me and the kids, you're wearing your oldest, rattiest T-shirt, and as far as I can tell you've been doing nothing but lifting weights since we came back. I have no idea what you did before that, but it sure wasn't cleaning up the house, which looks like a bomb went off. And, oh, yeah, we're having a party in a couple of hours. So, I repeat, what's wrong?"

Sometimes his wife just didn't know when to talk and when to leave it alone. "Nothing's wrong. I'll be ready when I'm ready. It's just a barbecue, for God's sake. Don't have a hissy fit about it."

"Hissy fit?" She started toward him, ready to rip his face off, he was sure, but she apparently thought better of it. "This is about Miranda, isn't it?" She sat beside him and put her hand on his leg. "Mark—"

"Her name's Ava, remember?" He switched hands and began curling with his other arm.

"It bothers you that Miranda changed her name."

He barely restrained himself from hurling the dumbbell at the wall. "Every damn thing about it bothers me. What's a little name change?"

She moved her hand from his thigh to his arm and patted. "Put that thing down and talk to me. Please, Mark."

Big, brown eyes beseeched him. He didn't want to, but he knew his wife. She wouldn't give up until he did what she wanted. Aiming to control his temper, he set the dumbbell on the floor and sucked in a deep breath. "I don't have anything to talk about."

"Of course you do. I know you're hurt and you don't understand why Mir— Why Ava won't or can't talk to you about what happened."

"Now why would I be upset? Just because my long-lost sister can't bother to come up with a good reason why she let us think she was dead all these years? No big deal."

"Of course it's a big deal, and she knows it, too. But the fact is, she's not going to talk about it. She either can't or she won't, and it doesn't matter which one, frankly. So you have two choices. You can continue to be angry and hurt and let her know it. If you do, you'll probably never get the chance to be a family with her again. At best, you'll be polite to each other when you run into one another, and the rest of the time you'll pretend the other one doesn't exist."

He shot her a sardonic glance. "What's my other choice, Madame All-Knowing?"

"Be as sarcastic as you want. You know what I'm saying is the truth."

He shrugged bad-temperedly. He wasn't about to admit she had a point.

Undeterred, Cat went on. "Your other choice is to accept her. Just as she is, without pushing her for answers. Start fresh from today and rebuild the relationship that was so important to you for all these years."

Still, he couldn't say anything. Maybe he wasn't ready to accept what Cat said was true.

She got up and look down at him, her eyes locked on his. "Think about it, Mark. What's the important thing here? Your pride? Or having a real relationship with the sister you thought was gone forever?"

He wanted a relationship with her. With Miranda, anyway. Ava…she was a different person. Or was she? Whatever had happened, whatever her reasons, she was still his younger sister. Sure, she'd changed, but then so had he. He still loved her and wanted to know her.

"What if I can't do that?" he asked gruffly. "What if I can't just forget it?"

"Then you both lose." She leaned over and kissed him. "But I don't think that's what you'll do." She hesitated before leaving. "I love you, you know."

"Yeah, I know." He caught her hand and pulled her to him, tugged her onto his lap. "I love you, too." He slipped his arms around her and kissed her.

Cat returned the kiss, then pulled back as he slipped his hand up to cup her breast. "No hanky-panky. We're having a party," she said severely.

"Not for hours. Where are the kids?" Her breathing quickened, which made him smile.

"They're at Jack's. He and Cole offered to keep them busy while we get ready for the party."

He tumbled her onto the bed and grinned at her. "So, do you want me to let you up?"

"Not yet," she murmured and pulled his head down to hers.

CHAPTER TEN

"DAD, CAN YOU COME HERE?" Cole yelled, loudly enough for Jack to have heard him in the next county.

Jack went into the den, where Cole and both of Mark's kids were. Cole and Max were sitting on the sofa, video controls in hand. He spied the problem as soon as he walked in but couldn't resist teasing the boys.

"Something wrong?"

"'Randa," Max said disgustedly.

Cole gave him a dirty look. "Can you do something with Miranda? We can't play our game. Every time we start she stands in the middle of the screen and blocks the view."

Jack laughed but went to pick her up. Luckily, her little hands weren't strong enough to have done any damage to the screen, but she'd been giving it a good try. "Come on, sweetheart. We'll go get a Popsicle and let those old boys play their games."

"Me too, me too," Max said as they left the room.

"In the kitchen," Jack told him, wondering if video games or food would win out. A few minutes later all three kids were in the kitchen with Popsicles, so obviously food played a major part in what the little ones thought important. Cole had always been a bottomless pit, so he wasn't surprised that Popsicles had lured his son away from the TV.

He wasn't surprised that Cole had agreed to occupy Max, either. Since he'd got up that morning and seen another car in their driveway, he'd been more pleasant than Jack could remember him being since he'd become a teenager.

Cole had stared at the small car for the longest time, then turned to Jack with guarded but ridiculously hopeful eyes. "Whose car is that?"

"Whose do you think?"

"It's mine?"

His voice nearly squeaked, reminding Jack of when it had changed. He smiled. "It sure as heck isn't mine. Happy birthday, Cole."

"Oh, wow! This so totally rocks! Thanks, Dad." He rushed out the door and got in, cranked the engine and turned up the car radio.

Jack had even got a hug out of it, and those had been few and far between lately. They were going to get Cole's license first thing after school tomorrow, so he couldn't take it out by himself yet, but Jack had gone with him to drive it around that morning. It was a small, economy model in a sort of off-green color, which wasn't the prettiest thing Jack had ever seen, but it ran, and that's all Cole cared about.

"How did you keep it secret?" Cole wanted to know.

"Hid it in Mark's garage." Which was how they'd ended up taking the kids for a couple of hours so Mark and Cat could get ready for the party. It had seemed like the least they could do for them.

Miranda was a beautiful child. Both the kids were, but Miranda was something else. Right now she was flirting with his son as only a two-year-old could do. Jack thought it was funny to see her wrap Cole around her little finger as firmly as she did her father.

He and Cynthia had planned on having more

kids. At least one more, they'd always said. But after Cole Cynthia had had a hard time getting pregnant and before they had decided to really pursue it, she'd had the accident.

He knew men his age and older who had young kids. If he ever married again… Suddenly Ava's face came to mind. He quickly shoved the image out of his head, knowing neither one of them wanted to go down that road.

But, damn, he thought about her way too much for comfort.

He realized the two younger kids had been throwing Popsicle sticks at each other. "Why didn't you stop them?" he asked Cole, going to pick up the mess.

"They were having fun. It's just a few sticks, Dad."

"And red, purple and orange splatters. Which you get to clean up."

"If we had a dog we could just let him do that." Cole sent him a sly glance as he said it.

Cole occasionally mentioned wanting a dog, but so far Jack had resisted. For a long time he'd figured that a kid was enough to worry about without having a dog added in. But Cole was plenty old enough to take care of a dog if he wanted to.

"We're not home that much," he said, testing the waters.

"Every night and most weekends. I'm here every weekend. You usually are."

"Dogs are a lot of responsibility."

"So's a car, and you got me one of those."

"Yeah, and if you're irresponsible with the car it can go away. It's not so easy to get rid of a dog. Would you want to take it back to the shelter?"

"We have a parrot," Max announced. "His name is Buddy. He talks a lot."

"I know," Jack said. "I've met him." Buddy was Cat's African gray parrot. According to Mark, she'd had to work hard to make sure he didn't utter some of his more colorful phrases around the kids. She'd been mostly successful, though Jack had heard Max utter a few zingers that he doubted the kid had learned from Mark or Cat.

"Dad, we were talking about a dog."

"Want doggie," Miranda put in. "Pease?"

"You'll have to take that up with your mom and dad," he told her. To Cole he said, "Are you willing to take care of it? Not just feed and water it but clean up after it and everything else that goes along with it."

His face lit up. "Oh, sweet. Can we get one, then?"

"You haven't said you'd take care of it."

"Of course I will. Let's go now!"

"Can I go?" Max asked. "I'll be good, I promise."

Jack laughed. "Sure you can, if it's okay with your parents. Let me call your dad and see if he minds if we take you and Miranda with us."

Jack was just about to leave a message on the machine when Mark picked up. He told him what he wanted and got the impression that Mark was more than happy to let him take the kids with him. Something told him that getting ready for the party wasn't the only thing Mark and Cat were doing.

"ARE YOU SURE you don't want a puppy?" Jack asked Cole dubiously.

"Well, yeah, sure I do. But look at him, Dad. If we don't take him no one will."

Jack sighed. Pretty, he wasn't. A three-legged mutt with the unlikely name of Lucky, the dog had laid its head on Cole's knee and was looking at him as if the boy was his last friend in the world. Which he probably was. But at least he

seemed sweet, and the people at the shelter said
he was good around kids and other dogs. Max and
Miranda hunkered down next to Cole and, patting
Lucky, obviously thought he was a good choice.

Crouching by the cage next to Lucky's, Jack
called softly, "Here, Princess." Chocolate-col-
ored, Princess was a Lab mix who looked to be
about six or seven months old. She came over and
pushed her nose against the chain link so he could
stroke it with his fingers and looked adoringly at
him with big, brown puppy dog eyes. Damn, he
should have known better than to come to a shelter
and expect to leave with only one dog. If they
didn't get out of here quickly he might even end
up with three.

"Can we see how she and Lucky get along?"
he asked the woman who'd showed them around.

"Of course."

Cole looked up. "We can have two?"

"If they get along. One dog might get lonely."

His son said nothing, just smirked as the two
dogs sniffed each other.

"What?"

"You're a sucker, Dad."

Princess snuggled against Lucky and rolled
over on her back for the kids to pet her. Jack

smiled. "Hey, if you can pick one, I should be able to pick one too."

"No argument from me," Cole said. "Look, they like each other."

"We'll take them both," Jack said. It was worth it to see the smile on his son's face. But if he'd known he wanted a dog so badly he might not have had to spring for the car.

AVA HAD JUST ABOUT talked herself out of going to Mark's party. She needed to unpack more, she reasoned, so that when she went back to work the next day she would be organized in her new home. Of course, she hadn't brought that much with her, preferring to leave most of her things in storage until she was sure if she liked the job or not.

No, she wasn't going because she couldn't face rejection, and she was certain by now that Mark would never forgive her.

Her phone rang. She checked caller ID and saw that it was Mark. Sucking in a deep breath, she answered. "Hello."

"Hi. It's Mark."

"Hi." Surely he wouldn't call to tell her not to come. Would he?

"Could you come over early?"

"To the party?"

"Of course, to the party."

"I…wasn't sure you'd want me there at all. Since you've had time to think about it, I mean."

"Don't be paranoid," he said, sounding exactly like the older brother she remembered. "We need to talk. I'll see you in a half hour, okay?"

"I'll be there."

She dressed carefully, if casually, in cool cotton slacks and a short-sleeved pink blouse. Checked her hair and makeup, then told herself to quit stalling. Straightening her back, she walked out the door. If Mark thought he'd push her out of his life now that she'd found him, he could think again. At least he wasn't going to do it without a fight from her.

THE NOISE COMING FROM inside Mark's house was deafening, even through the closed door. Several minutes after she rang the bell, then knocked, the door opened. Mark stood there holding a barefoot little girl on his hip and looking harried.

"Hi. Would you mind watching Miranda a minute while I go help Cat with Max?"

"Uh—" She knew nothing, absolutely nothing,

about children. Mark took her lack of response as assent, however, and handed the child over.

"This is your Aunt Ava, sweetheart. I'll be back," he told Ava and disappeared.

Miranda smiled at her, patted her cheek and started babbling. And Ava fell for her instantly. By the time Mark and Cat came in with their son, she and Miranda were fast friends. The little girl had led her all over the living room, pointing out toys and talking about the parrot, whose name was Buddy and who squawked, "Hello, sucker," several times at the top of his lungs. Apparently, Buddy had been the source of a good bit of the noise she'd heard.

"Hi, Ava. So glad you could come early so you could meet the kids. This is Max," Cat said, motioning to the dark haired boy who had his arms wrapped around her leg. "Max, this is your Aunt Ava."

He looked at her a bit suspiciously, she thought, but then he smiled. Oh, Lord, he was every bit as much of a heartbreaker as his sister. "Hi, Max."

"'Lo. How come I never met you till now? I know Aunt Gail and Uncle Cameron and—"

Mark interrupted before he could continue cataloging what seemed to be a long list. "We talked about this earlier, Max. Remember what I told you?"

"Oh, yeah. Are we gonna play ball at the party?" he asked his father, clearly losing interest.

"I'm sure you can convince someone to play. For now why don't you take Miranda and go play in your room for a while?"

Max seemed to consider debating that but apparently decided not to argue. "Okay. Come on, Miranda." The little girl followed him out of the room.

"Your children are beautiful," Ava said.

"Thank you," Cat said. "Why don't we sit down? It's going to get crazy before long. I have no idea how many people are coming."

Ava blinked. She couldn't imagine having a party and not having a clue how many people to expect.

"Cat has two brothers and a sister, so Max was going to be listing relatives forever," Mark said as they all took a seat. "You'll meet everyone at the party. As for our side of the family, Brian hasn't called me back yet, but I'm sure he will when he gets the message." He stopped, hesitated, then said, "I told Mom. She wants to see you."

Ava sucked in her breath. Jay had been adamant that he and Mark were going to tell their mother, so she shouldn't have been blindsided by the fact that they had done so already. But she was.

"Don't worry," Mark added. "She won't be here today. She and her husband are in Austin this weekend."

"I can't see her. I'm sorry, but I won't."

Mark's eyebrows drew together and she sensed his impatience. "Look, I had problems with her, too. So I understand, I really do. But as bad as it was, it wasn't all her fault. Jay said he told you about her illness."

"Yes, he did. But that doesn't absolve her from all responsibility."

"No, I know it doesn't." He frowned and rubbed the back of his neck. "Did she do something to you, too? Or was it just him?"

Ava closed her eyes. "She didn't do anything. That's the problem."

"I can't believe she knew what the bastard did to you that night. She wouldn't have condoned him beating you. No way. She'd have tried to stop him, I know she would have."

Ava opened her eyes and shrugged. "It doesn't matter. She abandoned us to that sadistic bastard and I for one can't forgive her."

"Mark," Cat said quietly.

He looked at his wife. She'd only said his name but they obviously shared a deeper communication.

"Okay, you're right." To Ava he said, "I'm sorry. I shouldn't have brought it up. Not now, anyway."

She just wanted to forget it. She might end up having to deal with her mother, but she'd put it off for as long as possible. "That's all right. I understand you feel like you have to try. But it's no good, Mark. I can't see her."

Mark nodded. "So, truce?"

She smiled. "You used to say that to me when we were kids."

"Yeah, I did." He shifted, looking uncomfortable. "I still don't understand why you didn't try to find us." When she would have spoken, he held up a hand. "But that doesn't matter. What's important is what happens now. We want you to be part of our family again, so we'll just forget the past until and if you're ready to talk about it."

"Do you mean that?"

"I wouldn't have said it if I didn't."

Feeling overwhelmed, she blinked back tears. "Thank you. It means a lot to me that you're willing to go with my wishes about this."

The phone and the doorbell rang at the same time. "Looks like it's started," Cat said. "I could use some help in the kitchen, Ava. How about it?"

"I'd love to," she said, and followed her sister-in-law out of the room. Family, she thought. She had a family again.

CHAPTER ELEVEN

IT WAS A GOOD THING Cat wasn't rehabbing any birds at the moment, Jack thought. If she had been, they'd only have added to the riot of sound the partygoers were making. Adults stood around in groups, talking. Children were running wild, dashing in and out of the groups of people. Somewhere in the background a boom box blared out some of the same kind of music he heard coming out of his son's room.

He made his way to the punch bowl, which was set up on a large picnic table that was already loaded down with food, from potato salad, to coleslaw, to beans, along with several unidentifiable casseroles people had brought. Mark was putting the burgers on the grill now. Good timing, since he was starving.

He saw Ava and, since she wasn't holding a drink, decided to remedy that. "Having fun?" Jack asked her, handing her one of the cups he'd picked up. "I've been trying to talk to you all afternoon but you've been surrounded by people."

She looked happy. More so than she'd been since he'd met her. She also looked a little bemused and bewildered.

"Yes, I am. Lots of fun. Thanks." She sniffed the drink, then sipped it. "What is this? It's good."

"Some punch Cat makes. Nonalcoholic, since she's pregnant. The kids think it's great."

"Yes, I've seen the evidence all over Max's face," she said, chuckling. "He's also managed to get red stains all over his father's shirt. Cat says he has a radar about that."

"Boys will be boys," Jack said, remembering that Cole at that age had been the same.

"Speaking of boys, I haven't seen your son, yet. Is he coming tonight?"

"I think he's still with the new additions to the family. He should be here shortly, though. He wouldn't miss free barbecue."

A couple of kids narrowly missed them with a football.

"Let's sit down before I get bashed in the head," Ava said, leading the way to an unoccupied table. "Tell me about these new additions."

"Dogs, two of them," he said, holding up his fingers. "And his new car. Well, new to him, anyway. Today's his sixteenth birthday."

She tilted her head and smiled at him. "You got him puppies *and* a car? That's awfully brave of you."

"Brave or stupid," he agreed, and he didn't know which of them was going to worry him more. Yes, he did. The car won, hands down. "I'm taking him to get his license tomorrow after school." Wincing, he pushed the thought of Cole driving out of his mind. Tomorrow was soon enough to have to deal with that.

So he went back to the animals. "One's a puppy. The other's grown." And Cole was already crazy about both of them. So was he, Jack admitted. He thought they were going to be fun. He couldn't think why he had resisted getting some pets for so long.

"I didn't realize you were such a soft touch. Of course, I met your son, so I can't blame you. Cole's a nice kid."

"Yeah, he is. Usually. He said you had him doing some work for you with the computer. How's that working out?"

She took another sip and smiled. "Wonderful, for me at least. It's tedious work, but he doesn't seem to mind. He's infinitely faster than I'll ever be." She shook her head. "It's a little…humbling. It took me months to learn this program—Fin-Scan, it's called. Dorsal fin recognition of dolphins. Cole had it figured out a couple of minutes after I showed him."

"He's good with computers and computer programs."

"I can see that. He's also been transforming analog pictures to digital for me so we can put them all online. That's even more complex. But he seems to like it."

He shot her a sideways glance before taking a sip of his own drink. "Could be it's the teacher he likes. He's been pretty full of 'Dr. Vincent said this' and 'Dr. Vincent does that.' I think he's got a crush on you."

Ava laughed. "Oh, please. I'm sure he thinks I'm ancient."

"I doubt that. He's no fool." She wasn't too old for Cole's father, not that he intended to mention that. No, she was just the right age for him. "Nothing wrong with appreciating older women. I'm glad to say he's got good taste." Before she could respond, he went on. "You look different. Happier. More relaxed."

She looked at him, considering. "I am, actually." She looked away, fiddled with her drink, then sighed. "Thanks for talking to me the other night."

"Not a problem." He waved a hand at Mark. "So, I'm guessing you all worked it out."

She looked at Mark, standing by the grill and talking to his brother-in-law, Cam. "Yeah, I think we did," she said softly. "I've got a family again. It's strange after all these years without one, but I think I'm going to like it."

Knowing it was none of his business, he stifled the urge to ask her about her past. One that had taken her so far from her brothers for so many years. Ava didn't strike him as the confiding type, anyway. As far as he could tell, she was a loner with a capital *L*. He had a feeling she'd already told him more than she was accustomed to telling most people.

He wasn't sure why she had. Maybe he'd just caught her at a vulnerable time. Which was odd in itself, since Ava Vincent didn't give off the vibes of a vulnerable woman. Anything but. Except for the other night, when she'd been so upset about Mark. Then she'd been hurting. And he had wanted, very much, to make it all better. *Not your problem or your business,* he reminded himself.

"What time do you want to leave tomorrow?" he asked, trying to rechannel his mind.

"Leave for what?"

He made a motion as if he were taking a picture. "Click, click. Pictures. You, me, the boat, the bay."

"I knew that," she said, and they both laughed. "Early, I guess. I'd like to have some time to upload the pictures into the program when we get back."

"Sounds good. We'll try to leave by eight-thirty, then. I need to get back early, too, since I'm taking Cole to get his license after school." He glanced at Mark, who was standing by the grill waving at everyone. "Looks like it's time for dinner. And surprise, surprise, here comes Cole. Talk about radar, that kid has one where food is concerned."

During dinner he and Ava became separated, but he sat close enough to watch her interact with her family. It must have been a little intimidating, he thought, especially for a woman who seemed so solitary. Mark's and Cat's families combined amounted to a whole bunch of people. Add to that mix who knew how many neighbors and friends and acquaintances, and you had a pretty imposing group. Especially when you didn't know any of them very well.

Ava seemed to be handling it okay, though. Or at least he thought she was until he saw an older lady corner her. After a short conversation, Ava began glancing around, clearly uneasy, but when she caught sight of Jack, her expression changed. If he hadn't known better he'd have thought she looked at him like he was her salvation. She said something to the woman, then hurried over to him.

"Help," she said.

He laughed. "What's wrong?"

"She threatened to introduce me to her nephew and Cat warned me about him. Not just boring but grabby and boring. And he's here tonight." She clutched his arm and started walking quickly in the opposite direction. "Get me out of here and I'll owe you a huge favor."

"I like the sound of that." He looked around a minute, trying to think of where they could go. "Come on," he said, steering her to the left. "I'll take you over to my house and introduce you to our new additions."

"I'd be willing to meet Jaws at this point."

They walked across the yard in the gathering twilight in a nice, companionable silence.

Unlike a lot of women, Ava didn't feel the need to chatter all the time. He liked that about her. Let's face it, he thought. He liked almost everything he knew about her.

"They're in the laundry room," he told Ava as he opened the kitchen door. "We checked the fence and there are a couple of places I'm not sure about, so we decided to keep them in here when we're gone, until I have the chance to fix it." Hopefully tomorrow evening.

"Are they housebroken?"

"I have no idea," he said, and opened the door. Standing in the doorway, he sniffed cautiously. "Don't want to curse myself, but I think they are." Both dogs looked up from the bed where they'd been snuggled together. Princess got up and bounced over to them while Lucky was a little slower to get up, but he hobbled over to them as well.

"Aren't you cute?" Ava said, leaning down to pat the enthusiastic dog. Lucky simply waited his turn, wagging his tail, until they both petted him too.

"Princess is the puppy," Jack said. "This one is named Lucky," he told her, scratching behind the dog's ears.

"What happened to his leg?"

"They didn't know. Could have been a car accident, or maybe cancer, though if that were the case he probably wouldn't have been abandoned. Why operate on a dog you're going to get rid of? The people at the shelter said he came in that way."

"It doesn't seem to bother him."

"I guess he's got used to it. He gets around fine on three legs."

She sat on the floor before he could stop her, letting the dogs crawl over her. "You're going to regret that. That floor's pretty dirty."

"Dirt has never bothered me. Look what I do for a living. You know it can be sweaty and dirty work."

"True." He sat beside her and pulled Lucky over to his lap. "But you're not usually wearing nice slacks out on the boat."

"They'll wash. And it's better than motor oil."

"Hey, I apologized for that. You never have given me the bill, either."

"No, and I'm not going to. Don't argue," she said when he would have.

"This isn't over," he said.

She ignored that, then glanced at him, her eyes

sparkling. "So tell me, Jack, which one did you pick?"

He grinned. "I fell for the girl. She was in the cage next to Lucky. I thought Cole would want a puppy, but he and Lucky bonded right off."

"I've never had a dog. Never had a pet, really." She was running her fingers over Princess's ears and the dog was sighing with pleasure.

"Never? Not even when you were a kid?"

She shook her head. "Our father…there's no way he'd have allowed us to have a pet. He'd have gone ballistic at the very mention of it."

"He was gone long before I knew Mark and Jay and Brian. But from what I gathered, your old man was a real son of a bitch. None of them talked about him much, but what they said made me glad I hadn't met him."

"That's too nice a term for what he was. Anyway, he wouldn't let us. You know I ran away. The people I lived with after that couldn't keep pets. She was allergic, so we never had any. After that I moved around a lot. Even once I stopped moving so much, I just never got one."

"You said you'd been married. You didn't have a pet then?"

"No. We both worked all the time, so it

wouldn't have been fair to the animal. Besides, Paul, my ex, didn't care much for animals."

She looked so content petting the dog, he said, "You could get one now."

Startled, her hand stopped and she looked at him. "Me? Get a dog?"

"Sure. Why not?"

"I…I live alone."

"No reason you can't change that. If you want. Your hours aren't that bad now, are they?"

"Well, no, but—".

"So nothing's stopping you. You could go after work tomorrow."

She stared at him a moment, then laughed. "You're moving way too fast for me. I'll think about it." She tilted her head. "What is this, you're a convert so now you're trying to convert me? You just got them today. You don't even know if you're going to like them."

"Sure I do. Admit it, you're tempted." He stood and reached down to give her a hand up.

She smiled, looking into his eyes. "You're right. I am tempted. Very."

Their gazes locked. Her eyes were gorgeous, a deep ocean-blue a man could drown in. His gaze dropped to her mouth. Full, sexy…beyond tempting. How long had it been since he'd kissed a woman, held a woman in his arms? Since he'd made love to a woman?

Too damn long.

"Jack—"

"I'm tempted, too," he murmured and kissed her. For a moment she didn't move, then imperceptibly, her lips parted. He took that as a good sign, and slipped his tongue over her lips, dipped it gently into her mouth. Her tongue flirted with his, then slid inside, tasting him as he tasted her. He dropped her hand and slid his arm behind her back, edging her closer.

He wanted to plunge in. Devour. And knew if he did he'd lose any chance with her. One last taste, one last flick of his tongue in that soft, sweet mouth, and he pulled back.

He thought she'd move away. Instead, she leaned forward, rose up on her toes and pressed her mouth to his again. He wasn't stupid. He kissed her back and the kiss deepened, turned hotter. He felt her melt against him and had wild thoughts of boosting her onto the dryer, stepping between her legs and seeing what happened.

Slow down, his conscious mind told him, but he really didn't want to.

Finally, when he was a heartbeat away from losing all caution, Ava drew back and stared at him, her eyes big, her mouth glistening. She started to speak but before she could, the kitchen door banged open.

"Dad, are you here?"

He dropped his arm, his gaze still on hers. "In here, Cole. I was introducing Dr. Vincent to the dogs."

"Sweet." He came in, oblivious to the vibes and to the way both of them looked. "Have you taken them out?"

"Sorry, haven't gotten around to it. Why don't you do that and I'll walk Ava back to the party."

"I think they're trying to get rid of everyone. Bye, Dr. Vincent. I'll see you Tuesday."

"Won't you be in tomorrow?"

Cole grinned. "Dad's taking me to get my license after school."

"Oh, that's right, he said he was doing that. Sounds fun. I'll see you Tuesday, then."

Neither spoke as they made their way back to Mark's, but this time the silence wasn't companionable. Tension stretched between them, a sexual awareness that seemed to grow with each passing moment.

They found Mark and Cat and said their goodbyes, then Jack walked Ava to her car. Neither mentioned the kiss they'd shared, though he'd have bet it was on her mind as much as it was on his. He opened her door and she slid in.

Leaning down he said, "How about that rain check?"

"What rain check?"

"When I asked you to dinner the other night and you couldn't come. The night you went to Mark's."

"I didn't say I'd go out with you."

"You didn't say you wouldn't, either."

Hesitant, she looked at him. "I like you, Jack."

"I like you, too. That's why I asked you to dinner. So what's the problem?"

"I'm not—I don't want to give you the wrong impression."

"Meaning what?"

"Meaning I don't think we should date."

"Why?"

She worried her lip before answering. "I'm a little burned out on relationships."

"Because of your divorce."

She nodded.

"And if I said it was just dinner between friends?"

She gazed at him a moment, then said, "Is that all you want?"

Lie or the truth? Since he'd just kissed her like there was no tomorrow, she'd see right through the lie. "No, but if that's all you're up for then I'm willing to go along with you." And try like hell to change her mind. He gave her his most winning smile. "Come on, Ava. What can it hurt? Tuesday, after work. I'll pick you up and we'll go over to Corpus Christi. It'll be fun."

"I don't know." She tapped her fingers on the steering wheel. "I suppose dinner wouldn't hurt."

"Don't look so apprehensive. You might even enjoy it."

"That's exactly what I'm afraid of," she said, and started the car.

CHAPTER TWELVE

"YOU'RE PLAYING WITH FIRE," Ava told herself Tuesday. She had no business making a date with Jack, even for something as innocent as a quick dinner after work.

That kiss they'd shared in his laundry room sure hadn't been innocent. She'd been a nanosecond away from losing whatever sense she had. Much more of that and she'd have found herself in his bed. All this, and it was only the first time he'd kissed her. Oh, Lord, she could be in big trouble here. She couldn't date, couldn't have a serious relationship. Her failed marriage should have proved that to her. That and the pitifully few relationships she'd attempted since then *had* proved it to her.

But she liked Jack. And she wanted to get to know him. She wanted… No, she wouldn't think about sex or how long it had been since she'd been with anyone.

She'd gone out on the bay with Jack again Monday. If anything, getting to know him better was only making him more appealing. None of that mattered, though. She had to nip this relationship in the bud. Make it clear they were friends and nothing more. He'd agreed to honor her wishes, but still… He'd admitted he wanted more. And damn it, so did she.

He was the first man she'd been really interested in since, well, she couldn't remember the last man. The first man who'd made her feel alive in years.

The phone rang as she was headed out the door, already late for work. Checking caller ID, she saw it was Mark so she picked up. "Hi, there."

"Hey, Ava. It's Mark. Do you have lunch plans today? Around noon?"

She felt a funny little thrill that she had family now. Family who cared enough to call. Her life right now was one new experience after the other. "No. Why, did you want to meet for lunch?"

"Yeah. How about the Scarlet Parrot?"

He sounded odd. Or was it just her, reading something into a simple invitation? She was so new to this, she didn't know. "All right." She hesitated, then asked, "Did you want to talk about something specific?"

"Why do you ask that?"

"I don't know. You sound sort of funny."

"Just meet me. We'll talk at lunch," he said, and hung up before she could get another word in.

"That was weird," she said, and replaced the handset on the charger.

Fortunately, she was busy most of the morning so she didn't have much time to brood over what was up with Mark or why she'd let Jack Williams affect her so strongly. It annoyed her, though, that what little free time she had she spent daydreaming about Jack. What was it about him?

Her phone rang and she snatched it up thankfully. "Ava Vincent."

"Brian Kincaid," he said with a laugh in his voice.

Brian. Oh, Lord, her heart nearly stalled. "Brian. Hi," she said, as if she'd talked to him last week instead of years ago. "Mark said you were going to call."

"Sorry it's taken me so long, but I've been out of pocket."

"That's all right. After all, it took me more than twenty years, so who am I to complain."

He laughed again and she knew they were

going to get along. They wound up talking for more than half an hour. He was still in China, so she knew the call was costing him a small fortune, but he insisted it wasn't a problem.

Talking to him wasn't nearly as uncomfortable as she'd expected. Brian seemed to be even more easygoing than Jay was. Of course, he'd been even younger than Jay when she left, so he didn't have many memories of her. Or maybe that was just his nature. She got the impression he didn't take a lot of things seriously.

By the time she met Mark she was very curious about what he wanted. They made small talk until they ordered. He pulled out two pictures drawn with crayon and handed them to her with a proud grin. "Max made me promise to bring them to you."

Her heart melted. She couldn't tell what they were supposed to be but he was only five, after all. "They're beautiful. Thank you. I'll hang them on my refrigerator." Another first. A picture from her nephew.

"That one's Buddy," Mark said, referring to his wife's parrot. "At least, I think it is. The other one is an elephant. He saw it at the zoo last Saturday."

She held both pictures up and studied them. "They're the same size. And the same color."

"Yeah, welcome to Max's world." He looked at them again and added, "Well, Buddy *is* gray."

She laughed and set them aside where they wouldn't get dirty. After their drinks arrived Ava sweetened her tea and waited for Mark to broach whatever he had to tell her, but he had fallen silent, tapping his fingers on the table. Exasperated, she finally said, "Okay, what is it? If I didn't know better I'd think you were nervous."

He grimaced. "It shows, huh?"

"What is it, Mark? What's wrong?"

"It's about Mom." He held up a hand. "Just let me talk before you freak out."

"I'm not changing my mind, if that's what you're asking. I won't see her." Hadn't she made herself clear? How many times was he going to ask her the same question?

"She's coming to town next weekend. She wants to see you so badly she would do anything to make that happen. Can't you put aside your bitterness enough to just see her? Even for a little while?"

"No." She put her hand on his arm, keeping it there until he looked at her. "I can't do it, Mark."

"You think I don't understand, but I do. I was the same way. She finally came to see me and told me the whole story. We worked through it, and believe me there was a lot to work through."

"The fact that you made up with her, that you forgave her has nothing to do with me. I haven't changed my mind. I don't believe she's any different than the self-centered woman I remember."

"You're wrong. I didn't believe it either, but she is different. She's loving and involved and…she cares, Ava. She cares a lot."

Pointedly Ava turned away, saying nothing.

"You're not the only one who went through hell, you know. So did she."

Ava stared at him. "You have no idea what I went through. No idea what my life was like. So don't tell me a sob story about our mother and expect me to buy it."

For a moment the tension was so thick you couldn't have cut it with a machete. Then before her astounded gaze, Mark started laughing.

"What? What in the world do you find funny?"

"You sound exactly like I did the first time Jay tried to get me to see Mom again. Exactly."

But Mark hadn't done what she had. He'd been honest and honorable, he'd taken care of his brothers when he was little more than a child himself. He hadn't left everyone to fend for themselves, like she had, like her mother had. He wasn't like her. And he wouldn't believe her even if she told him the truth about herself.

"Give Mom a chance," he said softly. "That's all I'm asking."

"Because I owe it to her? She's my mother, so I owe it to her?"

"You owe it to yourself. And yeah, you owe it to her. Bottom line is, she's our mother. She did the best she could under the circumstances."

Her best hadn't been good enough. But Ava knew better than to say that. "I'll think about it," she finally said. "But I want to get something straight. Whatever I decide, even if I decide I can't see her, you have to promise me you won't do this again. You have to accept my decision, and respect it."

The waitress arrived with their food and chatted with Mark a moment, then left them to their meal. She watched him start to eat, realizing he'd never answered her.

"Promise me, Mark."

"All right," he said reluctantly. "I promise I'll respect your decision, even if I think you're wrong. But you have to promise me you'll think about what I'm asking, not as a child but as an adult."

"What's that supposed to mean? Are you implying I'm being immature?"

"I'm not implying anything. I'm flat out telling you I think you're reacting as a child would react and not a grown woman."

Ava couldn't think of a thing to say.

"Don't you think Mom regrets what happened? Don't you think she regrets losing you?"

"I have no idea. I haven't seen the woman in over twenty years. But the woman I remember was too caught up in her causes and her own feelings to care about her children. She left me with him, Mark. She let him do whatever he wanted and didn't even attempt to protect us."

"You can't know that. We don't know what she said to him when we weren't around. Or what she tried to do to make things better for us. We don't know everything she endured from him, and we never will. She won't discuss it."

"It doesn't matter, does it? She failed us. Every one of us."

"Haven't you ever done anything you've regretted? Something you'd give anything to never have done or said?"

She closed her eyes as that shot went home. If he only knew. Forcing herself to remain calm, she looked at her older brother. "I said I'd think about it. Can we just drop this subject now?"

He grimaced but he didn't say any more about it. They ate in silence for a moment, then he said, "Has Brian called you? I finally talked to him this morning and he said he was going to call you."

"He did. It was…nice. Sort of strange, but nice."

"None of us see him very much since he took this job. I'm proud of him, but I wish he'd make it back to the States more often."

"You must miss him."

"Yeah, I do. But he seems happy jetting around the world and doing—" he waved a hand "—whatever it is he does."

"You're happy, too. You always wanted to work for the Fish and Wildlife Service. Cat said you used to work undercover busting animal smugglers but that you transferred to the office here when you married."

"Yeah. Undercover work's a little too dangerous when you've got a wife and kids. Plus you have to move around too much. But I like what I'm doing now."

"It's obvious you're crazy about them. Your family."

"They're the best," he said simply.

"You're lucky to have them."

"Believe me, I know that. Which brings me to my next question. Why aren't you married with some rug rats of your own?"

Her heart sank. She'd been expecting the question, if not from Mark, from Jay. "I was married once, a long time ago. It didn't work out. And children…they just didn't happen." And never would.

"You're still young enough to fall in love again. Get married again," Mark said. "It's not too late."

"Yes, it is. I'll never marry again." She clasped her hands together in her lap and made herself continue. "I…I can't have children."

He put his fork down. "I'm sorry. I didn't mean to be insensitive. Cat tells me I have no tact."

She smiled faintly. "That's all right. There's no way you could have known. But let's talk about something else." Please, God, anything else.

"Suits me." He ate another bite, then said, "I saw you go off with Jack at the barbecue. He's a good guy."

Okay, anything but Jack. "Yes, he is. But nothing's going on between us." *Just a kiss I can't forget.* Which was why she was going to break that date as soon as she got back to work. He was too dangerous to her peace of mind. "And nothing's going to go on, either, so forget about playing matchmaker."

Mark raised an eyebrow and smiled at her. "I never said I was. And speak of the devil." He waved and a few seconds later Jack strolled up to their table.

"Hello, Ava. Mark," he said, shaking hands.

"Join us?" Mark asked.

"Thanks, but I'm picking up a to-go order. I'm taking Dr. Long out on the bay this afternoon. Command performance. He's got someone he's hitting up for funds going along, too." He looked at Ava. "We won't be late, though. I can still make dinner."

Conscious of Mark's very interested gaze, she stammered, "I—I meant to call you. Something's come up and I won't be able to make it."

He looked a little surprised. "Okay. Want to try for tomorrow instead?"

"Um, I don't know about tomorrow. Can we talk about this later?"

He looked at her for a long moment and she

could tell exactly what he was thinking. She bet Mark could, too. He thought she was hedging and meant to break the date but was too chicken to come right out and say it. Which she was.

"Yeah, sure. See you around." He turned his back and went to the bar to pick up his order.

"Why did you do that?" Mark asked her. "Why did you break your date with him?"

She huffed out a breath, knowing she couldn't avoid answering. "He caught me at a weak moment and I agreed to go out with him. I've thought it over and decided it's not a wise move."

"Why?"

"Because it's not. I'm not interested in dating, and it's not fair to him to let him think I am." He was too tempting and she liked him too much for her own comfort. There was no point in going out with a man she really liked when she knew it would never work out between them. It wouldn't be fair to either of them.

"I don't get you. Jack's as nice a guy as you'll ever meet. Why won't you go out with him?"

"Mark."

"What?"

"Butt out."

He started to speak and then he closed his

mouth. "Okay, you're right. It's none of my business and you're a grown woman."

"That's right." She shot him a sideways glance. "I'd forgotten how bossy you were. And how nosy."

"I'm not bossy or nosy. Just concerned."

"Bossy and nosy."

He laughed. "Yeah, yeah. Point taken."

Despite herself, she couldn't help watching Jack, who was standing over at the bar. He was saying something to Cameron Randolph, Mark's brother-in-law and the owner of the restaurant. Jack never once looked her way. In fact, he left without even glancing at her again.

Which shouldn't have bothered her as much as it did. He was just a man. A nice man. Sexy. Appealing. Easy to talk to. But still, just a man. Nothing special, right?

Wrong.

CHAPTER THIRTEEN

JACK WAS STILL MAD when he took Ava out on the bay the next day. Not exactly mad, he realized with an unwelcome punch to his gut. Hurt and disappointed. Which was stupid and lame and made him feel like a loser.

So Ava had broken the date. Big deal. She didn't want to go out with him. He'd been rejected before. Hell, he'd been rejected lots of times. So what?

He still had to work with her. And he hadn't given up all hope she'd change her mind again. Okay, call him crazy, but he wasn't ready to give up on her totally. If he hadn't kissed her, if she hadn't responded the way she had, then he could have forgotten about it. Written her off as a pretty woman he'd never have a chance with. But there was no possible way he was going to forget that kiss or what she'd felt like in his arms. So, he would be patient.

He decided the next move was hers, though, so

he didn't say much as they cruised near the shore-line of the bay. He just let her work, clicking her pictures in silence. Surely she'd get sick of silence eventually and start talking.

It took her until late afternoon to finally say more than a couple of words. "We should talk."

"About what?"

She lowered the camera and looked at him. "You know what about. I know you're mad at me. You haven't said two words the whole time we've been out."

He shrugged without answering.

"I'm sorry I broke our dinner date last night."

"Are you?"

"Yes. But I warned you I wasn't interested in a relationship, and that's what dating leads to."

"I said we could be friends."

"You also admitted that wasn't all you were interested in," she reminded him.

"Fine." He scanned the waves for more dolphins, and when he didn't see any, slowed down. "Is this because I kissed you?"

"Don't be silly."

Was it? So why did she look flustered and uncomfortable? "It is. It's because I kissed you and you liked it."

She tossed her head and gave him a cynical look. "The ego speaks."

"You kissed me back." She didn't say anything. "Not ego, the truth," he continued. "Admit it, Ava."

She hunched a shoulder and looked away from him. "All right. I liked it. You're an attractive man and I'm a heterosexual woman. Are you happy?"

"I would be if you'd get over this idea that we can't go out."

She sighed. "I really don't think it's a good idea. And not because you kissed me. Or not entirely."

"What is it then?"

She bit her lip and looked out over the bay. "A lot of reasons. One of them is that I'm not up for a serious relationship."

"Who said anything about serious? It was a kiss. And then I asked you to dinner. That's not a damn marriage proposal, Ava. Not in my universe, anyway."

"Not in mine, either. But I…I like you, Jack. I don't want there to be bad blood between us. Which always happens, eventually."

"Not always. I'm not psychic. I can't see the future. Can you?"

"Of course not."

"Then you really can't say whether whatever's between us is going somewhere or not."

"It can't go anywhere."

He wondered why she was so adamant about that. "Why don't you just relax? We'll have dinner together and see where it leads."

Frowning, she narrowed her eyes at him. "That's just it. Going out isn't going to lead anywhere."

Man, she was a hard sell. "Okay, okay. We'll go to dinner as friends." She still looked doubtful so he added, "I won't hit on you." Not unless she wanted him to, and he intended to do everything he could to convince her she wanted him to. "Satisfied?"

"I guess," she said.

"So are we on for dinner?"

She continued to appraise him before she shrugged. "All right."

"That's not very gracious. Tell you what, instead of going out, you come to my house and I'll cook. How about it? I'll make one of Cole's favorites."

"What's that?"

"It's a surprise. Say you'll come. No fear of romance with a sixteen-year-old hanging around."

"Okay, you win. I'll be there. When?"

"Friday night. Seven."

"Sounds good." She looked at him a minute, then added, "Don't look so smug. It's just dinner."

"I know, but I like to win."

She laughed. Over her shoulder he saw something leap out of the water, heading into the small cove they were approaching. "Look, there's another pod of dolphins. At least, I think it's a different one. We're a lot closer to shore than we were this morning."

She raised the camera and started clicking. "It is a different one. See that dorsal fin? It's very distinctive. I can see a hole in it, thanks to my telephoto lens. I'm sure I haven't seen that one before. Four adults…and two babies, I think." She shot some more pictures then lowered the camera. "Why do they seem so agitated? Look, the mothers in particular seem upset."

"They've got company," Jack said. He motioned to a boat, a mid-size speedboat, that appeared to be heading straight for the pod. "They're protecting their calves." The boat wasn't slowing, if anything it sped up. "Don't those idiots know better than to crowd them like that?"

Ava put her hand on his arm. "Jack, they're

chasing them deliberately. I think they're trying to herd them into the shallows of that cove. We need to do something. We've got to help those dolphins."

"Crap. I think you're right." He started toward them, at the same time picking up the radio mike. "I'll call the Coast Guard. They're probably just stupid and wanting pictures and don't realize harassing dolphins is illegal."

"Hurry," she said.

"See if you can read the name of their boat." He got through to the Coast Guard, gave them the heading and a description of the other boat. "Hold on a minute and I'll give you the name." He turned to Ava. "Can you read it yet?"

Ava was leaning forward, straining to see. "I think it says…*Sunnyside*. Yes, that's it."

Jack relayed the information and signed off. "They said they'd be here but it might take a little while. At least they have the name of the boat and a description, so even if they miss them—"

Ava interrupted. "We have to do something. Jack, we can't just leave them alone. What if the Coast Guard doesn't make it in time? The dolphins could get stranded in the shallows. Or hurt, somehow. Oh, why are they doing this?"

It didn't sit well with him, either. To do nothing while those bozos tormented the dolphins. He angled the boat and kept going. "There's a chance I can cut them off and the dolphins can get out behind us."

"Do it." Her hand tightened on his arm as if she could will the boat to go faster. "We're gaining," she said. "I think we're going to—"

The other boat veered off as they approached, a little closer than he was comfortable with. Jack breathed a huge sigh of relief. He hadn't really thought the jerks would ram them, but they weren't exactly acting rationally. Probably drunk, if he had to guess. Definitely stupid.

"That was close," he muttered. "Jared would not have been happy with me if I'd wrecked the *Heart of Texas*."

Ava turned to him, eyes shining. "You saved the dolphins. Look, they're swimming out to the bay."

"That's a little strong, don't you think?" But it didn't hurt his ego to have her looking at him like he'd saved the world.

Frowning, he realized the other boat had turned back toward them and was picking up speed again. As he increased his own speed, going the opposite direction, he heard a crack of sound. For a full, heart-stopping beat he turned around and stared at the boat in disbelief and then he heard another sound, just as distinctive.

"Shit!" He shoved Ava down and, keeping one hand on her, pushed the throttle forward. "Stop wiggling. Stay down, damn it."

She wouldn't quit struggling and nearly sat up before he shoved her down again.

"What's the matter with you?"

"Haven't you ever heard a shotgun before?"

She stopped moving. "A shotgun? You think they're shooting at us?"

"Pretty damn sure. And I'd rather be wrong and feel stupid than blow it off and have a hole in me." Or worse, have her be shot.

"But—but that's ridiculous. Because we cut them off?" Her voice rose, strained with incredulity. "Are they crazy?"

He didn't bother to answer, being too occupied with saving their skins. He thought he heard the shotgun bark again but couldn't be sure above the sound of the engine. Glancing back, he was happy to see the other boat receding. They clearly didn't have the engine power of the *Heart of Texas*.

Their impromptu race seemed to last forever, but a few minutes later he recognized a Coast Guard cutter coming toward them, slicing through the waves. *Sunnyside* apparently saw it too because they turned again and took off in the opposite direction, away from shore.

His heart still beating uncomfortably fast, he eased back on the throttle. "The cavalry's here. You can get up now."

Her eyes huge, Ava rose to her feet and stared at him. "Those people—they were shooting at us? Actually shooting at us? With guns?"

"Well, it wasn't firecrackers." He reached across her and touched the canvas awning over the port side. "See this?" He fingered the small hole grimly. "Bullet hole."

Wrapping her arm around her stomach, she looked a little green. "I think I'm going to be sick."

He put his arm around her and pulled her against him, as much for his sake as hers. "Yeah, tell me about it. I don't feel so hot either."

The Coast Guard cutter pulled alongside them. "Lieutenant Braden," one of the men said, touching his cap. "And these are Ensigns Thorpe and White," he added, motioning toward the two men with him. "Did you folks call in about someone harassing dolphins?"

"Yeah." Jack pointed in the direction of the receding boat. "That's them. And the dolphins weren't the only ones they harassed. We got in their way, to let the dolphins head out of the shallows and I guess it pissed them off. They took a few pot shots at us."

Lieutenant Braden looked even more stern at that news. "Did they now? Anybody hurt?"

"No, we're fine. I found one bullet hole but haven't had a chance to see if any of the other shots connected. I heard at least two, maybe three shots."

"Don't you need to follow them?" Ava asked. "They're getting away."

"No, ma'am. Don't you worry. We've got another cutter set to intercept them. How about you give us a statement and we'll wait to hear from our officers on the other ship."

Jack and Ava told them what they knew, which was precious little. Not too much later Lieutenant Braden's radio squawked. He answered it, grunted a few times and then turned to them. "The suspects have been apprehended. Appreciate the heads-up. This isn't the first time some yahoos decided to bother the dolphins. Except this group's in for even more trouble, what with the shooting. Attempted assault with a deadly on top of a hefty fine for harassing the dolphins. They might even wind up doing some jail time."

"Couldn't happen to a more deserving group," Jack said.

"We'll be in touch if we need another statement. You folks take it easy." They drove off after promising to let them know what happened.

For a moment Ava and Jack simply looked at each other. Then she said, "I'm not usually a wimp, but that shook me up. Would you mind?" She stepped close, wrapped her arms around him and held on tightly.

He patted her back, happy to hold her, even if it was just for comfort. He tried not to think about how good that lush, curvy body felt against his. How good it would feel to kiss that soft, luscious mouth again. To run his hands over her curves. He failed, badly.

"Jack?" She eased away, still standing in his arms, but looking at him now.

"Yeah?" His voice was husky. He cleared his throat and stared into her eyes.

Her lips parted. She gazed at him as she leaned

into him. Fascinated, he lowered his head, intent on tasting those tempting lips.

She turned her head and stepped back. "I, uh—thanks. I needed that."

He forced himself not to grind his teeth. "Anytime," he said, with a lightness he damn sure didn't feel.

CHAPTER FOURTEEN

SHE'D GOT HER BREATH BACK, along with her senses. She couldn't believe how close she'd come to kissing him. Again. You'd have thought that kiss in the laundry room would have warned her how dangerous he could be. If she had kissed him, allowed him to kiss her… No, this way was best. For both of them.

Risking a glance at Jack, she saw he was looking thoughtful. She wasn't sure she trusted that look.

"That was a little too much excitement for me," she said, trying hard to dispel the sexual tension.

"I'm not a fan of being shot at either," he said drily, turning from her to start the boat.

So he was going to let it go, pretend, as she had, that the moment had never occurred. But she couldn't help wondering if it would be so bad if she did have an affair with him. Nothing serious, just…two people enjoying each other. What could it hurt, as long as they both knew the rules?

Too risky, she thought, and damned her cautious nature.

WHAT COULD HE MAKE that would blow her away but not look like he was trying too hard to do just that? He couldn't think of anything, so he did something he rarely thought about anymore and pulled out Cynthia's box of recipes. Thumbing through them, he crossed off a number as too difficult or too boring or impossible for him to make. Finally he hit on one he thought had real potential.

Coq au vin. It was perfect. And Cynthia's recipe was simple but looked difficult. Like he was a gourmet cook. Which he wasn't by any stretch of the imagination.

Friday he left work a few minutes early and stopped by the grocery to pick up chicken and vegetables. He had everything else he needed. Cole came in shortly after he got home while he was assembling dinner. "Hey, Dad."

"You're home early. What happened at work?"

"Dr. Long said to come in tomorrow morning so he let me leave early. 'Sup?"

"What's up is dinner. We're having company."

Cole peered into the pot dubiously. "Looks fancy. What is it?"

"Coq au vin. It's your new favorite meal."

"Huh? No it's not. My favorite meal is—"

"Doesn't matter." He chopped another carrot, scraped them off the cutting board into the pot. "You've got a new favorite dinner."

"So is this like, for a woman?" He picked up an apple from the basket on the counter and bit into it.

"Yeah. Dr. Vincent."

"Woo-hoo, go Dad!"

He flashed him a grin. "Glad you approve."

"I like Dr. Vincent. She's cool."

"I told her you'd be here. I meant to tell you before but I forgot."

His face fell. "Do I have to? A bunch of us were going to a movie."

It was Friday night, Jack reminded himself. He should have known Cole would have plans, especially now that he had his license. "Any girls happen to be going?"

Cole smiled. "Supposedly. They're meeting us there."

"All right." He was glad Cole was making

friends and doing something with a group. He just hoped they weren't the type to get into trouble, but for now he'd have to trust his son on that one. "I'll make you a sandwich before you go. What time's the show?"

"I need to leave here about seven-thirty."

"Okay."

"Thanks, Dad."

"Yeah, yeah." He picked up the spoon and waved it at him. "Don't be late, okay?"

"Yes, sir!" Cole gave him a cheeky salute. The phone rang and Cole pounced on it, walking out of the room with the handset glued to his ear.

Jack hoped Ava wouldn't think he'd engineered Cole being gone, but at least the kid would be there when she arrived. Shortly before seven the doorbell rang, just as he was grilling Cole's sandwich. "Get that, will you, Cole?"

He heard the murmur of voices and then they both came into the kitchen. "Hey, I won't be long. Just fixing Cole some dinner."

"You're not going to be here?" she asked Cole as she set a bottle of wine on the counter.

"I'm going to a movie with some friends. Sorry, Dr. Vincent."

"Call me Ava. I'm not really a formal person."

Cole shot a glance at his father. "If it's okay with Ava it's okay with me. Sit down, son."

"What are you making?"

"Grilled cheese. It's my specialty."

"I've never made it. Is that what we're having?"

He laughed as he slid the sandwich onto a plate and set it in front of Cole. "No, I'm making coq au vin for us."

"Yum," she said, going over to the stove to sniff the simmering dish. "Smells delicious."

"Mom used to make that," Cole said. "I remember she said it was her fa—"

Jack put his hand on Cole's shoulder and squeezed. "Your dinner's getting cold."

Cole looked at him a minute, then at Ava, and grinned. "Oh, okay. I get it." He finished the sandwich in a couple of bites. "Thanks, Dad." He put his dishes in the dishwasher. "Is it okay if I leave now?"

"Sure."

Sticking his hands in his pockets he hesitated. "Could I spend the night at Brad's?"

"Which one is Brad?"

"You know. Brad Abernathy. You met his dad last weekend. You said you liked him."

"I did. Are you sure his parents are going to be there?"

Cole groaned. "Yes, Dad. But I'll give you his number if you want to call."

"Thanks." But since Cole had volunteered the phone number it probably wasn't necessary to call. "Have fun."

"Thanks. Bye, Ava."

"Bye, have fun."

Jack stared after him. Maybe he should call, just to be certain.

"What's wrong?"

He shook his head. "Nothing. It's just…" He trailed off, not wanting to get into another discussion of the woes of single parenting.

"Going to a movie and spending the night out doesn't seem like something to worry a lot about."

"Ordinarily I wouldn't." He shrugged and turned back to the stove, stirring the savory dish before covering it again and letting it simmer. He crossed his arms over his chest and leaned back against the counter. "Cole got into trouble last year. It's why we moved. So I've had to be more careful to make sure he's doing what he says he's doing. And that parents are around. Parties without adults are an invitation to disaster."

"He seems like a good kid. Was it bad, the trouble he was in?"

"No, but only because I caught him before it had gone very far."

"Girls?"

"No. At least, I don't think girls are the problem yet. He got in with a wild crowd, experimented with pot. He said it was the first time."

"But you're not so sure."

He lifted a shoulder. "What parent ever is?"

"Not being a parent, I wouldn't know. But I can imagine how hard it must be having to do it all on your own."

"Sometimes it is. Especially when there are problems." He turned back around. "I think the worst thing is not having anyone to share responsibility with. But I didn't ask you over to hear about my kid and our problems." He pulled off the lid and got a fork out to give her a bite of the chicken.

"You said that before and I told you, I like your son. I don't mind listening to you talk about him." She sniffed delicately then took the offering. "Oh, this tastes like heaven. I thought you'd have red meat so I brought a burgundy."

"That's perfect with coq au vin, too."

She leaned against the counter and shot him an assessing glance. "So did you make this to impress me? I have to tell you, it's working."

He smiled. "Good. That was the plan." He got out a corkscrew and opened the wine, pouring two glasses. Handing her one he clinked his against it gently. "To smooth sailing and clear skies."

They both sipped their wine. "Was that a double entendre?" Ava asked.

"No. But it can be if you want it to be."

She laughed and shook her head. Jack stirred the chicken and put the lid back on. "It doesn't need much longer. Why don't we sit down?"

They both sat. He liked the way she looked at his kitchen table. Maybe too much. *It's just a date,* he reminded himself. Not a big deal. A platonic date at that. It's not like she was signing on to be the mother of his future children.

"Do you cook a lot?" she asked him.

"Some. Usually quick and easy stuff."

"I rarely cook. When I was young I had to make dinner for the family all the time. My mother…well, she was gone more often than not. So it fell to me. Mark tried but he was never very good. I usually just made sandwiches." She put her wine glass down and traced a finger around the rim. "The night I ran away from home, I made my father a turkey sandwich. Let's just say he didn't care for it and he let me know it. I haven't been able to look at one since."

"I'm sorry." He covered her hand. He was ridiculously pleased that she'd opened to him, even just a little.

Her gaze softened as she looked at him. "Thanks."

"You're welcome."

"Are you always so nice?"

He flashed her a wicked grin. "I wouldn't say I qualified for sainthood." Not if she knew what he thought about almost every time he saw her.

He patted her hand and got up. "Let's eat."

She got up and followed him into the kitchen. He popped the bread in the oven and quickly set the table. Topped their glasses off and pulled out her chair with a flourish.

"I can get my food. You don't have to wait on me," she said.

"I don't mind. Sit."

Looking a bit amused, she did. "You're very bossy, you know that?"

"Sorry. Comes from having a kid." He prepared

both their plates and set them on the table, then got the bread out of the oven and set it on the table as well.

"Dig in," he said, taking his seat.

"It looks wonderful." She took a bite and closed her eyes, obviously savoring the flavors. "And it tastes wonderful, too." She opened her eyes and smiled at him, her lips softly curving, her eyes luminous. "You went to an awful lot of trouble. Thanks."

"It was nothing." He stared at her a moment, watching her eat. Thinking how pretty she looked, wondering what it would be like if she was there more often. *Better watch out,* he told himself. She'd made it very clear she wanted no entanglements. And he had Cole to worry about. The last thing he needed was to get all twisted up over a woman. A woman who didn't want to get involved.

But damn, he was beginning to realize that *he* did.

CHAPTER FIFTEEN

AVA GLANCED OUT the window at Mark's house for at least the fifth time since she and Jack had started washing the dishes. Mark had said their mother was coming in from Dallas this weekend, but he hadn't specified which day. Not that she wanted to see her. She was simply curious. Who wouldn't be curious after all these years?

Her mother would be in her sixties now. It was odd to think of her as older since she remained frozen in her mind as the age she'd been when Ava had left, much as her brothers had until she met them again. She could still see her, slipping away and hiding from her husband, instead of standing up to him as Ava had always wished she would.

"See anything interesting?" Jack handed her the pan lid to dry.

He hadn't wanted her to help wash up but she'd

insisted. It had seemed like the least she could do after the wonderful meal he'd made for them. Not many men had cooked for her. Certainly not her ex-husband. He'd considered it torture.

Jack, however, seemed almost too good to be true. If that were so, though, why hadn't he married again after his wife died? She imagined that a lot of women would be willing to step into his late wife's shoes. He was a nice man, worked hard, loved his child. And the good looks didn't hurt a thing either. Still, he'd clearly loved his wife. Maybe he just wasn't ready.

She had a feeling when Jack fell, he'd want the whole thing. He'd had it all once, he would want it again. Deserved to have it again.

She glanced at Mark's house, dark and quiet. "No one's home," she said, realizing she'd never answered him.

"They're in Dallas. They went to see Mark's—I mean, they went to see your mother."

She dried the lid and set it on the counter. "Mark told me she was coming here this weekend."

"I guess she changed her mind."

Because Ava had refused to see her? Or maybe it had nothing to do with Ava. Lillian had a different life now, after all. A different husband, according to Mark. Whatever the reason, though, Ava was glad she didn't have to face her. "Mark and Jay want me to see her."

Jack stopped washing a moment and turned to face her. "And you didn't want to."

Ava shook her head. "Not only that but…I *can't* see her."

He rinsed soap off the pan and handed it to her. "I guess that's why they went there, then." He looked at her thoughtfully. "I know this isn't my business but I can't help thinking twenty some-odd years is a long time to carry a grudge. Have you thought about reconciling?"

"You don't understand."

"No, I don't. Why don't you tell me?"

She laughed. "You can't possibly be interested in this."

"I'm interested in everything about you, Ava."

He said it quietly, sincerely, and held her gaze as he did so. Searching his eyes, she didn't see judgment or condemnation. She saw compassion.

Maybe she should talk to Jack. God knows she needed someone to talk to and she sure as hell couldn't talk to her brothers about their mother. Because Jack wasn't family, he didn't have an emotional stake in the whole process. She needed objectivity and Jack could supply it.

"If you're sure you don't mind… I think I'd like to talk to you about it."

"I wouldn't have offered if I didn't want to hear it." He poured them each another glass of wine and picked them up. "Let's go in the den. We'll be more comfortable in there. Or at least, we will if Cole picked up his video games and controllers like I told him to."

She took a seat on the couch and Jack sat beside her. She started to lean back but something hard poked her in the small of her back. Reaching behind her, she pulled out a video game controller.

"Sorry. I guess he missed that one." He took it from her and set it on the coffee table.

Sipping her wine, Ava thought about how to start. Obviously, she couldn't tell Jack everything but she had to tell him some of it if she expected him to understand.

"Do you get along with your parents?"

"Most of the time. They moved to Colorado several years ago, so I don't see them very often. They come here for holidays and I've sent Cole to stay with them during the summer several times."

"Did he go this summer?"

"No, we moved instead."

"What about when you were young? Did you get along with your parents then?"

"We had the usual arguments. Nothing major." He chuckled reminiscently. "I was an only child and they were pretty easy on me. Except there were a few times when I really made my dad mad." He shook his head. "Not a smart thing to do."

She hadn't considered she might be probing his old wounds. "Did he hurt you?"

"Hurt me?" He stared at her, then said slowly, "You mean did he beat me? You think I'd send Cole to him if he'd been abusive?"

"It happens."

"Not to me, it didn't. My father is nothing like that. He just made me really sorry I screwed up. Ashamed, and sorry I'd disappointed him. It's a nice trick. I wish I had it with Cole."

"Are you sure you don't?" she asked, momentarily diverted from her point.

Jack shrugged. "I can make him sorry he did something by grounding him, but I'm not sure about the sorry he disappointed me."

"Maybe you're too hard on him. He's a good kid, Jack."

"I never said he wasn't." He snapped it out, clearly irritated.

Ava decided she'd be wise to drop the subject. No one liked their parenting skills called into question, especially by someone who didn't even have children. "So you'd say you had a nice, normal family life?"

"Yeah." He paused a moment before adding, "I know you didn't."

"My father was abusive. And my mother knew it."

"Abusive how?"

"Verbally, for the most part." Until that last night. "I don't know what he was like after I left, but Mark and Jay told me he didn't beat them. I don't imagine he quit verbally abusing them."

She bit her lip and continued. "My mother knew all this. She knew how he was and instead of throwing him out, she tried to placate him. When that didn't work, she escaped and left us to deal with him. She was always working for some charity and leaving us at home. Especially after she had Jay and Brian. Mark and I were always babysitting. Our father would come home and hit the roof that she was gone. He'd take it out on us. Especially Mark."

"I'm not saying your mother was right, but maybe she was afraid of him. A lot of women are afraid to leave their abusers. If he was whaling on her she might have been afraid he'd kill her if she tried to leave."

"I don't think he hit her, either. I never saw it anyway. No, he was emotionally abusive. Not physically. At least, not until the night I left." She forced herself to meet his eyes. "He beat me black and blue with his fists at first, then he got out a belt. For the finale he kicked me and broke some ribs. He damn near killed me. I don't know how he didn't."

Jack looked sick and angry. "You mean to tell me your mother was there when he beat you? And didn't do anything? Didn't try to stop him?"

"No, she was gone as usual. No one was home. Mark would have protected me if he'd known. Or tried." But thank God, he'd been gone. She knew what their father would have done to Mark if he'd tried to interfere.

"So she didn't know what he'd done to you."

"I don't know." Grimacing, she rubbed her temples. It was impossible to say what her mother had known or hadn't known. "Mark says she didn't. None of them did. And my father sure wouldn't have told them."

"Maybe you should hear her side of it. I have to tell you that as a parent I can't think of anything worse than my child running away and never being heard from again. God, that's a horrible thought."

"You're not like my mother. You're obviously a good father. It's clear in everything you do that you're crazy about Cole."

"I love him, sure. But I make mistakes. A lot of them. I think part of the reason he got in with a bad crowd was because I was working all the time." He closed his eyes for a moment, then opened them. "I can't tell you how guilty I feel about that."

"Why did you work all the time? Didn't you want to be with your son?"

He looked shocked. "Of course I did. I was trying to support us. The charter fishing business is time consuming, if you're successful."

"But you quit. And took another kind of job. You did something about the problem. You moved and changed jobs so you could be there for your son. Didn't you?"

"Well, yeah. But I'm his father. I'm all he has. I'm supposed to be there for him."

"Not everyone does what they're supposed to do, Jack." She knew that better than anyone.

"I think most people do. If they can. You don't really know what went on with your mother. For your peace of mind you might consider finding out. I think you're waffling and you just need a good reason to go ahead and see her. Hearing her side of the story might be that reason. And maybe you need to tell her your side of what happened, since you never have."

"I'm not waffling. I told Mark from the first I wouldn't see her."

"Then why are we even talking about it?"

She eyed him irritably. Coming back to Texas and finding her brothers had stirred up emotions she thought she'd put away. She hadn't realized how much anger and resentment she still carried toward her mother because she hadn't been forced to think about her until now. "I really hate this."

"What, that you think I'm right?"

"Yes. It's very annoying."

He took her hands, gave them a comforting squeeze. "Think about it. You don't have to do anything now. If it was your father, I wouldn't be arguing with you. I'd think you were crazy if you wanted to see him again. But if you could reconcile with your mother, or at least meet with her and let her see you, I think you'd feel better. Otherwise it's going to haunt you for the rest of your life. It already has, hasn't it?"

"That's not what haunts me." The words were out before she could stop them. Horrified at what she'd nearly let slip, she jumped up and paced to the window, turning her back on Jack.

A moment later, she felt his hand on her shoulder. "What does haunt you, Ava?" he asked quietly.

She let her head fall back. God, talk about a quick end to a budding relationship. All she had to do was tell him her history and he'd run so fast the other way she'd get windburn. And though it might be the best thing, she wasn't ready for what they had to be over.

She didn't want it to be over, she realized, because she wanted more. More than friendship, she wanted to be lovers. Which was about the worst thing she could do, but that didn't change what she wanted.

"I can't talk about it."

"If you ever want to—"

"I don't." She turned and looked at him. "You don't know me. You don't know what my life was like. It was nothing like what you have with your son. Nothing like what you had with your wife."

"What I had with her wasn't perfect."

"Maybe not." The question came out before she could stop it. "Are you still in love with her?"

"With Cynthia?" He looked surprised, then smiled, a tender, loving smile. "I'll always love Cynthia. But it's been six years, Ava. I'm ready to move on."

He was looking at her as if she had all the answers. Worse, as if she *was* the answer. "Be careful what you ask for."

"Because I might get it?" he asked, his voice deep and husky.

He was close. So close she could feel his breath, warm and inviting against her lips. Almost as if he were kissing her. She wanted, badly, to kiss him. Wanted to forget, for even a moment, what she'd done.

What she'd been.

"Stop me now," he murmured.

She should. She knew she should, but she didn't.

He framed her face with his hands. His mouth lowered, his eyes locked with hers, then he captured her mouth and kissed her. Long, slow and deep.

She didn't fight him. Didn't resist. Instead, she put her arms around his neck and kissed him in return. His tongue entered into her mouth, sure and steady, stroking, taunting. Her heart rate sped up as he pulled her closer, as his hands fell to her hips and pressed her tightly against him.

She dug her fingers into the hair at the back of his neck and kissed him for all she was worth.

They stumbled to the couch. Her legs bumped against it then she sank down into the deep, over-stuffed cushions. Jack followed her, lying heavily on top of her with his thighs between her parted legs. He brushed her hair aside and kissed her neck, wet openmouthed kisses that made her breasts throb and tingle, her blood heat.

Murmuring against her neck, he said, "I haven't had a woman get me this hot, this quick in—" He laughed. "I can't remember when." Easing away from her, he watched her face as he slipped a hand under her shirt, dipped his fingers inside her bra to flick them against her nipples. Then he pushed up her bra, cupping and stroking her breast.

It felt wonderful. She didn't want to stop. For once she wouldn't think about the consequences. She tightened her legs around him and thrust her pelvis up, feeling him hard and tempting in the cradle of her thighs. He groaned and pressed against her, then he kissed her again, his tongue driving inside in a clear rhythm of desire.

He rolled on his side but before she could protest, his hand reached down and cupped her between her legs, stroked her there. She wanted so badly to feel his fingers dance along her naked skin. He must have wanted that, too, because she felt him unbutton then unzip her pants.

"Ava." He pushed his hand beneath the waistband of her panties, and she felt his finger slide over her slick, wet heat. She gasped as he slid it inside her and withdrew it, then did it again. "I want to make love to you."

"I want you, too." His thumb stroked her as his finger probed, she tensed, ached, her muscles tightened as he drove her higher.

Their breathing was labored. They stared at each other. She wondered what he was waiting for. Why he didn't make love to her there, or take her into his bedroom.

"I want you so badly," he said. "And I really, really don't want to ask you this."

"Ask me what?"

"Are you sure this is what you want?"

CHAPTER SIXTEEN

SHE STARED AT HIM, lips parted. "Are you having second thoughts?"

"No." He shook his head and groaned out a laugh. Then he rolled off her and helped her to sit beside him, taking her hands between his. "Hell, no. But I don't want you to regret this. It's too important to me. You're too important to me."

She looked at him for a long, silent moment. "I'm no good at relationships, Jack. I have a failed marriage and…and there are other things. If you're looking for happily ever after, I'm not the woman to give it to you."

"I don't know what I'm looking for. I just know that you're the first woman since Cynthia died who's…been this important to me."

"Jack, are you saying you haven't been with anyone since your wife died?"

He smiled a little at that. "No, that's not what

I'm saying. There have been women. Not a lot, but enough for me to realize that what I feel for you is nothing like what I felt for them."

"Don't."

"Don't what? Tell you I'm falling in love with you?"

She turned her head and said in a choked voice, "Don't. You can't."

"Sorry. It's too late, I already have."

She looked at him then. Man, she had some gorgeous eyes. "I'm not the woman you should fall in love with."

He put his arm around her, pulled her closer and kissed her jaw. Moved upward and kissed her mouth, at the corner. "Too late," he said again and covered her mouth with his.

For a moment, she resisted. Then her body softened, leaned in to him and her mouth answered his. "This is a mistake," she said, pulling away.

"If that's what you really think, then why are you here?"

"Because I'm tired of fighting it."

"Fighting what, Ava?"

She sighed, wrapped her arms around his neck and kissed him. "I'm tired of fighting what I feel for you. Tired of fighting what I want."

"What do you want, Ava?"

Solemn as could be, she looked at him. "Take me to bed, Jack."

He didn't make her ask twice. Swinging her up in his arms, he headed for his bedroom.

ALONG THE WAY she lost her shoes and had started on the buttons of her shirt before he carried her into the bedroom, kicked the door shut, then set her on her feet and backed her up against the door.

"I wanted to take this slow," he said hoarsely. "But I don't think I can."

"I don't want slow. I want fast and hot and soon." She attacked his buttons, pushed his shirt off his shoulders and spread her hands over his wide, tanned chest. "Mmm," she said, and kissed him there.

A laugh rumbled in his chest. "I know what you mean. What is it about you that makes me want to eat you right up?" He wrestled with the rest of her buttons, dragged her shirt off and tossed it over his shoulder, then popped her bra clasp, ripped it off and threw it down as well.

She laid her head back against the door and closed her eyes as he cupped her bare breasts in his work-roughened hands. "That feels...so good."

She opened her eyes and watched him. "I've been thinking about this, almost since I met you."

"Me, too. I think about you all the time." He bent his head and licked her nipple, then drew it slowly into his mouth and sucked. She speared her hands through his hair and held him closer. "All the time," he murmured, swirling his tongue over her nipple.

He raised his head, kissed her mouth as he lifted her up, and she wrapped her legs around him, feeling his arousal through their layers of clothes. How much better would it feel when they were both naked?

Jack must have been thinking the same thing because he swung her around and strode toward the bed. They tumbled onto it and she reached for his zipper, struggling to slide it down as he fumbled with hers. He stripped her jeans and panties off, then stopped to look at her, intense appreciation in his gaze. Then he rolled aside and shoved his own jeans down his legs.

He opened his nightstand drawer and pulled out a thin Mylar packet, tossing it on the tabletop. For a man who said he hadn't been with many women since his wife died, he kept those suckers mighty handy.

"I bought them the other day," he said, as if reading her mind. "The day we were shot at, on my way home."

"You planned this. Tonight. You planned to get me into bed, didn't you?"

"No." He kissed her, skillful, deep, amazingly slow, until she relaxed.

What did it matter? She was here with him now and that was exactly where she wanted to be.

Finally, he broke the kiss and murmured, "I hoped. Which is entirely different from planning."

"Entirely," she said, laughing, and pulled him into her arms and kissed him.

He palmed her, slid a finger inside her. She was damp, aching, and she wanted him inside her now. She grasped his erection and stroked, gently at first, then harder.

"It's been a long time for me," he said huskily.

"For me, too."

He rolled aside, grabbing the packet and opening it, then sheathed himself before returning to her. "Now," she said, opening her arms.

He came inside her in one smooth stroke, withdrew, then drove back in. She moaned as he thrust gently and withdrew, then did it again, and again, each time harder, stronger, deeper. Her muscles tightened and her orgasm burst like a star, furiously intense.

He muttered something, maybe her name. He kissed her, then raised his head and pushed inside her one more time, filling her, surrounding her. His muscles clenched, he groaned harshly and spent himself within her.

She almost passed out but the heavy weight was welcome. It took her a minute to realize Jack was crushing her into the mattress, but she didn't say anything. It felt good. So good. A feeling she'd almost forgotten.

"I don't want to move," she said.

"I don't either." He groaned and rolled off her. "But I know I was suffocating you." He wrapped his arm around her and snuggled with her, spoon fashion. "Can we stay like this forever?"

Ava laughed. "I don't think so. What about your son?"

"What son?"

"Funny, funny. What about food? We'd starve to death if we never left the bed."

"You have a point. Okay, we can have a break for food. But we can only eat it in bed."

"That might work. Except I hate crumbs in bed."

Cracking open his eyes, he raised himself up on his elbow to look at her.

"What?"

"I was just thinking how beautiful you are. And how good you look, naked in my bed."

She smiled, pleased by the compliment. "You don't look so bad yourself."

He kissed her neck, gave her a love bite and soothed it with his tongue. "Next time we'll take it slow."

She didn't, as she had in the past, say something evasive, then get up and leave. No, she wanted to pretend, if just for a minute, that everything would work out and she could have a lasting relationship with Jack.

So, she turned her head and kissed him, long and lovingly. "Slow would be good. But fast was good, too. Very good."

CHAPTER SEVENTEEN

AVA LEFT VERY EARLY the next morning, long
before Jack expected Cole to be home. Before she
left, they'd decided to eat at her place that night
and she'd told Jack to bring Cole if he didn't have
other plans. Then Jack had kissed her senseless
and let her go.

As she left, she glanced at Mark's house,
feeling a familiar twinge of guilt that she couldn't
do what her brothers wanted her to do and reconcile with their mother. Maybe Jack was right and
if she at least saw her mother she might find some
peace in that relationship.

Right now, though, she wanted to be with Jack
and enjoy him and try not to think about any
problems. She should have run the minute he'd
told her he was falling in love with her. But she
hadn't. What did that say about her?

Maybe he was wrong. Maybe he just thought

he loved her, when in reality it was just the sex he needed. But she knew that wasn't true. She'd been very aware that the sex meant more to each of them than just a way of scratching an itch. That it was far more than a one-night stand.

She'd gone and done exactly what she'd sworn not to do. She'd fallen in love with Jack.

THEY SPENT THE WEEKEND together, some of it with Cole, some alone. She'd been a little afraid that Cole might resent her, that he might view her as trying to usurp his mother's place, but he seemed fine with his father dating her. And he was a great kid. The more time she spent around him the more she realized that regardless of his concerns about raising his son, Jack was a good father. And he tried harder than anyone she'd ever seen.

Certainly more than her own father ever had. She couldn't remember so much as a kind word from him, much less a genuine show of love.

It was Sunday afternoon and raining and Jack and Cole were playing a video game. Shouting, groaning, laughing as one won a point over the other. They looked so much alike, she thought.

Jack looked up and smiled at her before Cole's

shout of triumph warned him he'd given away his advantage.

"I'll get you for that," he warned his son. "I have a secret weapon."

"Ha! Last time you said that I scored the most points I ever had."

"That was a different game. This is football. I know football."

She tried to picture her father playing a game, any sort of game, with one of his sons. She couldn't. He'd never thrown a ball with them, never played a board game. Never read to them. Never attended a school function, as far as she knew.

Her mother had read to them. Ava had buried that memory, one of the nice ones. Lillian had read to all of them when they were small. And she'd gone to Ava's softball games, as well as the boys' sports events. At least, until the last year before Ava left, their mother had tried to give all of her children some of the attention their father wouldn't. Eventually she'd quit, as if she'd dried up under the weight of her husband's abuse. Then she'd discovered the charities, and they had consumed all of her time.

But she hadn't always been that way. Ava let

herself recall some of the good days. Days when their father hadn't come home and made them all miserable. When their mother had played with them and sang to them and loved them. Before she'd become an empty, desperate shell of a woman. Before her husband had destroyed all her hopes and dreams with bitter words and endless accusations.

It didn't justify what had happened later. What she'd allowed her husband to do to their children. Nothing ever would, Ava suspected. But could she take that first step to see if a reconciliation was possible? Call Mark and tell him she wanted to see their mother?

Not yet. But maybe, just maybe she would do it soon.

OVER THE NEXT couple of weeks Jack and Ava spent a lot of time together. She and Cole really liked each other and from what Cole let fall about work, she was teaching him a good bit about marine mammals. Cole had been interested in them from a young age, but Jack hadn't thought his son would actually go into a career in that field. He was beginning to think he might now, though.

And it might have been because his own personal life was going so well, but Jack thought Cole was adapting to Aransas City better than he had dared to hope. His son wasn't sullen or cranky anymore. Or no more so than any normal teenager. Cole had friends now, a group of guys and occasionally girls who came over and ate everything in sight and tossed around the football, watched movies and played video games. They weren't perfect, but most of them seemed like nice kids. There were one or two Jack had met who he suspected weren't quite as angelic as they'd have their parents believe, but Jack hoped Cole had learned his lesson and wouldn't be drawn into doing anything stupid again.

Cole seemed to like work, as well. Especially since a stranded dolphin had come in and he'd been able to help with its rehabilitation. He'd talked of nothing else for days.

So Jack's life was about as settled as it ever would be with a teenage son. He hoped that before long it would become even more settled, though. But first, he had to talk to his son. Alone. And since Ava wasn't coming over for a few hours, tonight seemed like the perfect time.

"Have any plans after dinner?" he asked Cole after he got home from work.

"I have a math test tomorrow. I was gonna go study with Andy. He aces all his tests and he said he'd help me with the algebra."

"Better him than me," Jack said. "But can it wait for a while? I'd like to talk to you after dinner."

"Am I in trouble?"

"No. Why, have you done anything you should be in trouble for?"

Cole shrugged. "Nothing I can remember." He paused. "But you know my memory sucks."

Jack laughed. "Too true. It's about me, not you."

"Why don't you tell me now?"

Because he was nervous. If he was this nervous talking to Cole what would he be like when it came time to talk to Ava? "All right. Let's sit in the den."

Cole followed him in there, saying, "What's up, Dad? You're being kinda weird."

They sat on the couch and Jack fumbled for a way to begin. "You know I've been seeing Ava a lot over the past few weeks." *Duh,* he thought, when Cole just looked at him. "You like Ava, don't you?"

"Sure. She's cool."

No sense beating around the bush. "What would you think if I asked Ava to marry me?"

"No shit?" He flushed and said, "I mean, no joke?"

Jack nodded, deciding not to take issue with the language since he figured the kid had a right to be surprised. "I've been thinking a lot about marrying her. But I wanted to make sure you were okay with it before I asked her."

"You mean you wouldn't ask her if I said no?"

Jack frowned, wondering how to phrase his answer. "I wouldn't marry someone I didn't think you could accept. Or someone I didn't think would love you, too. You know you're important to me, Cole. You're the most important person in my life."

"I guess. Except now she is, too, right?"

He smiled. "Yeah, she's important. You don't seem to have any problems with Ava, not that I've seen, anyway. And I know she likes you."

"No, I like her fine. That's not it." He fell silent for a minute. "But marriage is kind of a big deal, isn't it? And you haven't known her very long. How do you know you really want to marry her and it's not—" he spread his hands "—well, you know. Not just all about sex. I mean, Dad, your love life has been pretty lame since Mom died."

How he kept a straight face, he would never know. Being lectured by his son on confusing lust and love was something he'd never thought he'd experience. Still, it was a valid question and deserved an honest answer. "It's true we haven't known each other long. And yes, marriage is a big deal. But as for knowing it's for real, I knew with your mother almost from our first date."

Remembering that, he smiled. It was a good memory, and one that didn't hurt as much as it once had. "I've only loved two women and I made up my mind real quick with both of them."

"You sound pretty sure."

"I am, son."

"We'll have to be polite all the time. Women are big on that," he said wisely. "My friends' moms are all the time telling them to be polite. No burping or scratching and stuff like that."

Jack laughed. "Yeah, we'd have to change a little. Not be such slobs. But she might cut us some slack since we've lived without a woman around for so long."

"Will she want to make the house all girly?"

Looking around, he tried to see the place from a woman's perspective. "Maybe a little. I'm sure there will be things she'll want to change. But she won't do anything to your room."

"Good, 'cause I don't think I'd like that. Andy's mom puts girly stuff, you know like lacy crap, everywhere. Every stinking chair in their den has some lacy thing on it. Andy doesn't like it but she cried when he told her that so now he pretends he likes it."

"Maybe we can negotiate on the lacy crap. Besides, I don't think she's big on lace. I haven't seen any at her house." He stopped, aware they were drifting from the point. "But we're kind of getting ahead of ourselves. I haven't asked her and she hasn't said yes."

"But you think she will."

"I hope so. Like you said, though, we haven't been dating very long." He'd never even told Ava he loved her, and she hadn't said it either. But he didn't think he'd misread her feelings for him.

Cole jerked him out of his reverie with his next question. "Dad, are you gonna have more kids?"

He laughed. "Now that's *really* getting ahead of ourselves. Why don't we worry about that some other time. At least until we find out if she's going to marry me." For one thing, he didn't know if Ava was childless by choice or if she simply hadn't had a chance to have children. They'd never discussed it. Come to think of it, there were a lot of things they hadn't discussed. "Would you mind?"

"I don't know. It'd be weird, having a brother or sister so much younger than me."

"Like I said, let's not worry about it yet. And Cole, don't say anything to Ava. I'm not sure when I'm going to talk to her."

"Okay, but what are you waiting for?"

"The right moment." He rubbed the back of his neck. He'd know it when it happened, wouldn't he?

Cole studied him. "If you say so, but I think you're nervous."

"You could be right." After all, it was only the second time he'd ever wanted to marry anyone. A man had a right to be nervous about asking the woman he loved to marry him.

CHAPTER EIGHTEEN

AFTER TALKING TO COLE, Jack had a hard time not asking Ava to marry him the very next time he saw her. But he was worried she might think he was moving too quickly, so he decided that he should lead up to the subject. Give her time, get her used to thinking about it instead of firing off the question out of the blue. With that in mind, he asked her to come to dinner Friday night at his place.

He decided to make spaghetti sauce and noodles. It was one of Cole's favorites, but he was going out with his friends. So Jack and Ava could have a nice, romantic dinner with candles and wine. He was even using the nice dishes instead of the chipped everyday ones.

He tuned in to a classic rock channel on the boom box he kept in the kitchen and started to get down to business, taking out the ground meat and crumbling it into the sauce pan. As it cooked he chopped onions and garlic, then sautéed them as soon as the meat had browned. He added more spices, tossed in tomato sauce and let it simmer, the longer the better.

He was cleaning up, singing along with Mick to "Sympathy for the Devil" when Cole came in shouting for him at the top of his lungs.

"Dad, Dad, come quick!"

"What? Calm down, Cole. What's wrong?"

"I don't know! There's water coming out of the ceiling fan in the den!"

He barely remembered to turn down the stove top burner before he ran out.

By the time Ava arrived, a couple of hours later, he hoped the evening could be salvaged. "Hey, you look great," he said, kissing her after he opened the door.

"Thanks. What's going on?" she asked. "I see the plumber's truck is here."

"Don't ask. The water heater broke and I've had to get a new one, but they should be finished soon. We'll eat once they leave."

"I take it the dogs helped," she said, glancing around the kitchen.

"Yeah, they had a great time. How did you know?"

"There are muddy paw prints all over the floor," she said with a smile. She took off her jacket and hung it on the coat rack. "At least you had sense enough to hire a plumber instead of trying to do it yourself. I remember one time my ex-husband decided he was going to fix the leak under our kitchen sink. It was a disaster and cost us twice as much as if we'd hired the plumber in the first place. Not to mention, after he broke it, he went off to play golf and left me to deal with it."

He smiled, deciding not to mention the call he'd put in to Mark. "That's the first time you've mentioned your ex since you told me you were divorced."

"Is it?" She looked surprised, then shrugged. "There's really not much to talk about. We were married briefly a long time ago. I haven't even set eyes on him since we filed for divorce. I don't think about him very often, just when something reminds me of him."

"You don't sound bitter."

"I suppose I was, once. But it was for the best. We should never have married in the first place."

He walked to the kitchen and she followed. "Why?" He admitted he was curious. Had the dissolution of her marriage been as easy as she made it sound?

She crossed to the stove and sniffed the simmering red sauce. "Smells delicious. I love spaghetti. Did this come out of a jar? It looks homemade."

"It is. Take a bite, and you can tell me if it needs anything." Obviously, she was trying to change the subject. "Would you like a glass of wine?"

"I'd love one."

He poured them both a glass and handed one to her. "You don't want to talk about your marriage."

She took a sip of wine then asked, "Why are you so interested in my marriage?"

He leaned back against the counter and considered her. "Because we've never talked about it. We've talked about mine, but you've barely mentioned yours."

"Therefore you should know all about mine."

Her voice was flat and he thought there was more than a note of irritation in it. "It was a simple question, Ava. Nothing for you to get angry about."

"I'm not angry. But has it occurred to you that

I might not want to talk about my failed marriage to someone who so clearly had a good one?"

He stared at her a minute, then said, "No. I'm sorry, but it didn't."

She glared at him. "How can you be so nice when I'm being so unreasonable?"

He started to answer but the plumber called his name from the other room, so he had to go take care of him and the bill. When he returned, Ava was standing at the stove, stirring the sauce.

Turning around, she smiled at him. "I'm sorry."

He went to her, hugged her and kissed the top of her head. "Don't worry about it. I'm sorry I brought it up."

After they'd finished eating, Ava laid down her fork and looked at him, her eyes troubled. "Do you really want to know about my marriage?"

"Only if you want to tell me about it." Which was a lie. He wanted to know, but he wouldn't force her to talk about something that was painful to her, no matter how much she protested that it wasn't important.

"His name was Paul. Paul Baxter. We were young, both in our early twenties. When we married, he promised me…something. Then he changed his mind. So we divorced."

"What did he promise you, Ava?"

She looked away. "He swore to me that he didn't want children. The only way I would marry him was if he promised that not having children wouldn't bother him. He promised, so like a fool I believed him. Then a couple of years later, he met someone else, fell in love with her and got her pregnant." She snapped her fingers. "Poof, no more marriage. He slapped me with divorce papers so fast it was ridiculous."

He covered her hand and squeezed gently. "That must have hurt. Why didn't you want children?"

"I *can't* have children. Which I told Paul when he started talking about marriage."

"Are you sure? You were awfully young. Maybe the doctors—"

She interrupted, her tone flat and final. "Dead sure. I had to have a hysterectomy."

Jack stared at her, at a complete loss for words. "God, Ava, I'm sorry," he finally said. "No wonder you didn't want to talk about it."

She shrugged off his sympathy. "He knew what he was getting into when we married. Just as he knew I wouldn't agree to adopt, either."

"What's wrong with adoption?"

"Nothing, for other people."

"How can you categorically say you wouldn't adopt a child? I've seen you with Cole. It's obvious you like kids. I don't understand."

She simply looked at him. Her gaze was unfocused, as if she was in a different place, a different time. "I don't deserve children."

"That's a crazy thing to say. Of course you deserve children. If you want them. Why would you say that?"

"Because it's the truth." She leaned forward and glared at him. "You asked for the story and I told you. Don't blame me if you don't like what you hear."

"I don't like for you to bash yourself by saying something like you don't 'deserve' children."

She got up, carrying her plate to the sink then turned around to look at him. "You don't know me, Jack. I'm not like your wife. I'm not the wonderful human being she apparently was."

"Where did that come from? I never said Cynthia was perfect, or that our marriage was perfect." He took his own dishes, dumped them in the sink, then grasped her arms and looked down into her face. "I'm not comparing you to her, if that's what you think. You're a completely different woman. I'm glad you are."

"You have no idea how different we are."

Nothing she said was making sense to him. "Are you trying to pick a fight? What's wrong, honey? What are you upset about?"

"Nothing, damn it!" Twisting away from him, she took off for the other room.

He followed, grabbing her arm before she reached the coat rack beside the front door, which she was clearly headed for. "Ava, wait. Don't leave like this. Something else is bothering you. Tell me what it is."

For a long moment she stared at him, and then the fight visibly drained out of her. "It's not your fault. I'm upset and I'm being a bitch and taking it out on you." She laughed homorlessly. "I warned you I wasn't a nice person."

He ignored the comment, though he wondered if she really believed she was so bad. And if she did believe it, why? "Come sit down and tell me what's going on."

Still concerned she might take off, he kept hold of her hand and led her to the couch. "What is it?"

Using her other hand, she massaged her temple. "I took your advice and now I'm having second thoughts."

"What advice?"

"I called Mark and told him I'd see our mother. She's coming to town tomorrow."

"And you're freaking out."

"Pretty much. I'm sorry I took it out on you."

"Don't be so hard on yourself. I convinced you to talk about your marriage and you didn't want to. I should have just let it be."

"It shouldn't be such a big deal. I said I'd see her. I didn't promise to forgive her or anything else. Seeing her again shouldn't matter so much."

"She's your mother. Of course it matters."

"She hasn't been my mother in more than twenty years." She paused. "But lately, lately I've been remembering some of the good times. Before she grew so distant." She shook her head. "Let's watch a movie or something. I don't want to think about this anymore. There's nothing to be said that hasn't already been said. I just have to wait and see what happens."

He let her choose a movie and put it in the DVD player, then turned the lights down low and settled back on the couch with his arms around her. Definitely not the time to propose. And given what she'd said about her first marriage, he was less optimistic that she'd accept when he did ask her.

CHAPTER NINETEEN

AVA HAD ASKED MARK to bring Lillian to her house. She hoped that wasn't a mistake, but she thought being on her own turf would be to her advantage. Which sounded like she was fighting a battle.

Well, wasn't she?

Her doorbell rang. Sucking in a deep breath, she reminded herself that all she had to do was see her mother. Nothing else. That's all she'd promised. She opened the door.

"Hi," Mark said. The woman beside him—their mother—held his arm as if it were a lifeline. She stared at Ava mutely, her eyes brilliant with unshed tears. Ava suspected she wanted to hug her, but she was in no way ready for that.

"Do you want me to stay or come back later?" Mark asked Ava. He glanced at their mother and smiled.

The smile held not a trace of bitterness. Ava realized he truly had forgiven her.

Ava didn't answer immediately. *She's so small,* was her first thought. She had almost forgotten Lillian was so petite. Ava had inherited her height from her father, one of the few things he'd given her she didn't mind.

Lillian's hair was blond, like Jay's and Brian's, and casually cut in a short, feathery style that suited her. Her eyes, a beautiful blue she'd passed on to Mark and Ava, still glistened with tears. She wore classic black slacks and a thin black sweater that made her look even smaller than she already did. She could have passed for ten years younger than her true age.

Opening the door wider, Ava stepped back. "I think we'll do better alone. But thanks."

"All right." He bent to kiss Lillian's cheek and gave her a supportive hug. "Call me on my cell phone when you want me."

"Thank you," she whispered and walked inside. She stood staring at Ava, looking lost and alone, her white-knuckled hands clutching her purse in front of her.

"I don't know what to say to you," Ava said. "I thought I would, but I don't."

"I know this is…difficult for you. Thank you for—for letting me come. It means more to me than I can possibly tell you."

Again, Ava got the impression that her mother wanted to hug her. Why did she feel mean because she wasn't ready to let her do that? When she'd already taken a huge step in simply seeing her.

"Let's sit down. There's no reason to stand around like this." Ava took a seat in the overstuffed chair, letting Lillian sit on the couch beside it.

"You're so beautiful," her mother said, her voice cracking. "You were such a pretty child, I knew you'd be beautiful when you grew up."

"We can cut the small talk," Ava said, determined to take control of the situation. "Did Mark tell you why I ran away? What happened that night?"

Biting her lip, Lillian looked down at her hands and nodded. "Yes, he told me what you'd told him and Jay. Your father beat you and he threatened to hurt your brothers. Rather than face him again, you ran away."

"I ran for my life. I knew he'd kill me the next time," Ava said flatly.

Lillian's eyes met Ava's. "I didn't know. You may not believe me, but I swear, I didn't know. If I had, I'd have—" she faltered to a halt.

"You'd have what? Just what would you have done if you'd realized he beat the hell out of me? Left him?" She fired the words like bullets and her mother jerked back in shock, her expression anguished. But Ava couldn't stop and she pressed on. "Emotional abuse is okay but beating your child isn't? Is that it?"

She looked as if Ava had hit her. "Miranda—"

"My name is Ava now," she interrupted. "Don't call me Miranda. Miranda Kincaid doesn't exist anymore." That girl had died long ago, her innocence destroyed.

Lillian whitened further and closed her eyes. "I'm sorry, I forgot. Mark told me." She drew in a shaky breath and started again. "Ava, you have every reason to hate me. I should have left your father. But I was afraid. And I didn't understand, not until years later, what he'd done to you children. I thought—I thought I was his main target, I didn't realize how bad it was for you children."

Hadn't she? Or was that an excuse? "Jay said you were sick. That you were hospitalized for depression." She didn't want to feel sympathy for her mother, but she did.

"Yes, but not until later. After your father left. And it doesn't matter. What matters is I let you down. I let down all my children, but especially you."

Ava didn't comment because it was true.

"When you ran away, when the police couldn't find you, I thought you were dead. I wanted to die. But I didn't. I had private detectives look for you, against your father's commands. But I didn't leave him, I couldn't. Even though it was horrible living with him, I was scared to leave. Afraid to be on my own, with the boys to take care of. I don't know what would have happened if your father hadn't left us, but I thank God every day that he did."

"I still don't understand why you stayed with him. I'll never understand why."

"There's no simple answer. But—I thought I deserved his treatment of me. It took me years of therapy to understand why I allowed him to treat me that way. It wasn't until I married Walt that I knew what a good marriage was and just how truly bad my first one had been."

Years of therapy, depression, even hospitalization while she fought to get her life together. Her mother hadn't come out of the marriage without scars. She must have felt as helpless as Ava had, as battered by circumstance as Ava had been. It hadn't really sunk in until now that Lillian had been a victim, too. Ava had known it intellectually, but she'd never felt that kinship with her mother until this very moment.

"You'll never forgive me, will you?" Lillian asked quietly.

"I…don't know. It's too soon." But she wanted to. For the first time, she wanted to let go of the past. Could she have a relationship with her mother, as well as her brothers? Only if she allowed it.

"Mark said some people took you in. They adopted you, informally."

"The Vincents. Yes, they were wonderful. They saved my life. Literally."

"What happened?"

Ava shook her head. "I can't talk about it."

"Over the years I tortured myself with what could have happened to you. I was so thankful to hear you found someone to help you. Someone who loved you."

"Do you expect me to apologize for not letting you know I was alive sooner?"

"No. I'm well aware that you hate me."

Did she? Perhaps once she had, but no longer. "I don't hate you. Even though you stayed with him, at least you weren't the monster he was." Unwillingly she added, "I know what it's like to be helpless. To think you have nowhere to turn, no other alternative than the nightmare facing you." To have to depend on strangers, who were only looking out for their own interests. If it hadn't been for the Vincents... God, no, she couldn't think about that. She'd spent the last twenty-three years desperate to forget it.

"Oh, Ava. I wish you didn't. With all my heart I wish you didn't." She leaned forward. "I understand why you haven't wanted to see me. But why didn't you try to see your brothers? They loved you so much. Mark especially, since you were so close in age. It killed him when you ran away."

She'd kept her secret for more than twenty years. She meant to go on keeping it until she died. "I can't tell you. But trust me, I had a very good reason."

"I'm so sorry. Sorry for the time you missed with your brothers and sorry for my part in causing it."

"I'm sorry, too." To her surprise, she was. "I've blamed you all these years, but it wasn't all your fault. I have to take responsibility for—for what happened. For my life, and the way I've lived it."

"I love you," Lillian said. "I've always loved you. I thought of you every day of the last twenty-three years. Not a day went by that I didn't think about you, miss you and pray that you were safe and happy. To know you're alive, to see you, here in the flesh… It's a miracle." She buried her face in her hands and sobbed.

Despite her reservations, the sound of her mother's weeping tore at her heart. "Don't cry." She reached out, touched her knee tentatively. "Please don't cry."

Lillian looked up, wiped her eyes. "I'm sorry. I'm just so happy you're here. That you're alive and well."

She couldn't bear to look in her mother's eyes without giving her something to comfort her. "I'm glad I decided to see you."

"You are? Really?" Lillian's face lit with hope.

Ava nodded. "I really am. We can't have our old relationship back. I wouldn't want it back. But maybe we can forge a new one."

"I hope so. I want that more than anything. To

know you again, spend some time with you." Lillian held out her hand and Ava grasped it. "A new beginning."

"I want that, too." And the past could stay where it belonged. Dead and buried. Yet never, ever forgotten.

JACK HAD ASKED AVA to call him after she saw her mother. He wanted to be there to offer her support if she needed it. He hoped like hell the two women worked something out. He was beginning to get worried when his phone finally rang around two o'clock.

He snatched it up, reading caller ID. "How did it go?" he asked. "Are you all right? Do you need me to come over?"

"No, I'm fine. It went…surprisingly well. She's not like I remembered. Jay and Mark were right about that. I think she really has changed."

"That's good. I'm glad for you."

"Me, too. I'm wrung out, though. Even though it turned out better than I'd expected, it was emotional."

"I bet. Do you want to talk about it?"

"Maybe later. It's…a lot to take in. I need some time to think."

"All right. Are we still on for dinner?"

"Jay asked us to dinner at their house. They're having the whole family, except Brian, of course. I know Jay's trying to make sure my mother and I see more of each other, but having other people around should make it easier."

"Okay. But you don't have to ask me. It's a family thing. I understand that." He could live without seeing her one night. He didn't like it but he could live with it. They'd been together almost constantly since they'd made love for the first time.

"I want you there, Jack. Please."

No way would he turn down that request. "Okay, if you're sure."

Since Mark had been estranged from his mother when Jack knew him before, he'd never met Lillian Monroe and her husband, Walt, until that evening. Walt was a nice guy in his mid-sixties who laughed a lot but not in an annoying way. He liked Lillian as well, and it was clear the rest of the family had put their differences behind them.

After dinner the whole group of them sat around Jay's living room talking. Or trying to talk. With Jay and Gail's three kids, Mark and Cat's two and two very large mixed-breed dogs, who somehow managed to be inside over Gail's protests, it was difficult to hear anything.

"Are you okay?" He leaned over and spoke in Ava's ear, since otherwise he couldn't be sure she heard him. She looked bemused and slightly uncomfortable, as if she didn't quite fit in with the noisy group.

"I'm fine. A little out of my depth." Ava glanced at her mother, who had Miranda in her lap and Jay's two daughters, Roxy and Mel, at her feet. She was leaning on her husband's arm and laughing at something the toddler was doing. "It's so weird to see her like that. With grandchildren who obviously love her. Children she's close to. You can tell."

"She's changed. You said it earlier."

"Yes, I just didn't realize quite how much she'd changed. It's like she's a different person."

"I like Walt. He's a good guy."

"Yes, he is. She told me that he convinced her to try to reconcile with Mark and Jay and Brian years ago. Said she wouldn't have had the courage before she met him."

"She loves you. You can tell by the way she looks at you. Like you're a miracle she can't quite believe is really here."

"I'm no miracle," she said. "Far from it."

"What do you mean?"

Startled, she stared at Jack as if she'd forgotten he was there. "Nothing. It's not important."

Maybe. But if it wasn't important why had she looked so upset? So terribly sad? "Do you want to go home? We can talk if you want."

"Thanks. But there are some things you can't talk about."

Even to the man who loves you? He wanted to ask, but he didn't.

CHAPTER TWENTY

"THANKS FOR COMING WITH ME tonight," Ava said after they arrived at her house.

"I enjoyed it. I like your family."

"It's strange to have a large family again after so many years without any family at all." She moved around the den, straightening cushions, turning down lights.

"I'm sure it is. There are a lot of them to deal with. My family's so small, it's just me and Cole and my parents. Cynthia's mother died several years ago and her father died when she was just a child, so Cole only has the one set of grandparents."

"That wasn't all of them," she said with a laugh. "They didn't ask Mark's and Jay's in-laws. I think they thought it would freak me out to have even more people to deal with."

"Would it have?"

She shrugged. "I don't know. Probably. Even though Mark and Jay have tried so hard to welcome me, I still feel out of place. Especially with…my mother. Having you there made it easier for me."

"Any time." He tugged her into his arms and kissed her.

He drew back and cupped her cheek, looking deep into her eyes. "I mean that. Any time you need me, I'm there. All you have to do is ask."

"Then," she said huskily, "I'm asking." She smiled and kissed him. "I want to make love with you, Jack."

"You don't need to ask me that twice."

He followed her to her bedroom, watched while she lit the bedside lamp, pulled down the bedcovers. Watched while she unbuttoned her shirt, drew it off and laid it over a chair. She wiggled out of her jeans, a move that never failed to arouse him, then crossed the room to where he was standing.

Taking his hand, she led him to the bed and had him sit. Put her hands beneath his T-shirt and pushed it up, over his head, then tossed it on the floor beside them.

Stepping back, she kept her eyes on his as she

took off her bra, then slipped out of her panties. Already aroused, the sight of her made him hard as granite in no time.

"Are you seducing me, Ava?" he asked, watching her slick her tongue over her lips in a deliberately arousing move.

"That's the plan." She offered him a wicked smile. "Unless you have an objection."

He groaned and lay back as she went to work on his pants. "I'll let you know if I think of one."

"Have I mentioned I really, really like your body?" Finished with his clothes, she straddled him and kissed her way down his chest.

"I don't…know," he managed to say. "But I know…I like yours." His mind was clouding. He could barely remember his name, much less the question she'd asked him. Then she slid off to continue down his body, her lips and hands smooth and hot, her dark hair like satin falling over his chest, tickling, arousing. She kept going, her mouth soft, tormenting, driving him over the edge.

"Come here," he said hoarsely. "I can't last any longer." He grasped her arms and pulled her on top of him.

She rode him, lost in ecstasy, her eyes closed,

her cheeks flushed, her hands on his chest. He pulled her head down, kissed her mouth as he thrust inside her and came with a roar of satisfaction, then he felt her shatter around him, heard her cry of completion.

"Ava." They were still locked together, Ava collapsed on his chest. Neither had moved but she raised her head and looked at him, a soft, satisfied smile on her kiss-swollen mouth. He brushed his knuckles against her cheek. "I love you."

Her eyes widened, focused on his. Her gaze was unbearably sad. She put her fingers on his lips and whispered, "Don't. Don't say it."

When he would have spoken, she kissed him. And then she made love to him all over again, until he couldn't think, could only feel steeped in her, surrounded by her scent. Lost in love with her.

"IT'S LATE." Jack groaned and sighed into Ava's hair. "I have to go."

She lay snuggled against him, flat on her stomach with one arm thrown across his chest. She didn't want to move. "Don't go."

"I wish I didn't have to." He kissed her mouth,

then rolled over and got up. "But I have an impressionable teenager at home, remember? I can't call him and tell him I'm shacking up at my girlfriend's. Not if I expect him to listen to any of my lectures."

Some men would have, but not Jack. He was so determined to do the right thing for his son. To teach by example. If that meant denying himself something he wanted, then he did it willingly.

He stepped into his jeans and fastened them. He picked up his shirt, pulled it over his head, then sat beside her on the bed. Putting his hand on her back, he stroked her slowly before he spoke. "We have to talk about it, you know."

"Talk about what?" she asked, though she had a sinking feeling she knew. He looked at her so solemnly, his sandy hair falling over his forehead, his eyes dark and intense. She wanted to take her hand and push the lock of hair back, soothe him because she knew he wouldn't like—or understand—what was coming.

"We have to talk about the fact that I told you I loved you, and you didn't want to hear it."

Oh, God, why did he have to bring it up? Why did he have to say he loved her at all, much less mean it? Because she knew he wouldn't have told her if he hadn't really loved her. Jack didn't lie, he didn't evade, he didn't keep secrets. No, she was the one who did that.

She had to be hard-nosed about this. The last thing she could afford to do was let him suspect for an instant that she loved him, too. Because if he knew, he wouldn't understand why they couldn't stay together, why there could never be a serious relationship between them. A man like Jack wanted marriage, family and that would never be possible with her.

She got out of bed and grabbed her robe, wrapping it around her and belting it carefully, while she considered what to say. "I see no reason to complicate what we have with declarations of love."

"What the hell is that supposed to mean?"

Wishing she smoked so she had something to do with her hands, she walked away from him, trying to look casual. "We have a good time together. We enjoy each other. We have good sex. Why complicate the matter?"

His jaw tightened. Good, she thought, watching him. If she pissed him off maybe he'd drop the subject.

"We have fantastic sex. And I'm complicating *the matter*..." he said, stressing her last words sarcastically "…because I've fallen in love with you, Ava. Are you saying you're not in love with me?"

She tossed her hair back and faced him, willing herself to be strong. "No, I'm not," she said, lying through her teeth. "I like you, Jack. You're a great guy. But love just isn't possible for me." If her heart broke into tiny bits at the lies she uttered, so what? Knowing she loved him would only make it worse for him in the long run.

"All this is to you is sex." He gestured at the bed, to the sheets, twisted and falling off the bed. He took three steps, coming to stand in front of her, backing her up against the dresser. "Good sex, I think you said."

Raising her chin, she looked him in the eye. "That's what I said."

He moved even closer. "Tell me again," he said, his gaze unwavering, as if he knew she lied simply by looking at her. "Look at me and tell me all we have is sex."

She couldn't say the words. Instead she looked away, afraid she would cry.

"You're lying," he said, very quietly. "I want to know why."

She twisted away from him, putting her hands to her temples and squeezing, anything to stop the tears that threatened. "Goddammit, Jack, leave it alone! I told you from the first I didn't want to hurt you. Don't make me hurt you any more than I have."

"Answer my question," he said, his voice soft but implacable. "Were you lying when you said it was just sex to you? Do you love me, Ava?"

"Yes!" she shouted. "Damn you, yes."

"I don't understand."

She gave a wretched laugh. "I know." She walked over, put her hand on his arm. "Please, Jack, can't we just forget we ever had this conversation? Can't we go back to the way we were? We were happy."

He was staring down at her, troubled. "No. I can't leave it alone. I want more. I was waiting for the right moment, but this is going to have to do. I love you, Ava. I want to marry you."

Oh, God, it just kept getting worse. Despairing, she closed her eyes. "I can't," she finally forced out. "Don't ask me because I can't."

"Why? Because you had a failed marriage years ago?" he demanded. "You were twenty-something years old when that happened. That's no reason not to try again if you love me and I love you."

He'd never give up. And she could never tell him the truth. "The reason my marriage failed is why I can't marry you. I told you I'd never marry again. It was a mistake, and I won't ever put myself, or someone I care about, through it again."

"Why?"

She didn't answer and he continued, "Because you can't have children? Is that what all this is about?"

Desperately, she latched on to what he'd said, though it was only part of the reason. "You deserve a woman who can give you all the children you want."

"What I deserve is a woman I love. And that's you. I don't care about having more children. I have a child. Or we could adopt. Or not adopt. I don't care, Ava. I just want you. To marry me and be a family with me and my son."

"No, you don't. You don't know me. You think you do, but you have no idea who I am. You know nothing about me." He didn't know what she'd been, what she'd done. He'd hate her if he did.

"Of course I do. You're beautiful. You're kind and loving and smart and funny. You love basketball and fall colors and spaghetti and meat sauce and when you're working hard you get a look in your eyes that tunes out the rest of the world. And when you're loving me," he said, his voice dropping, "your eyes get blurry and your mouth softens and you're so beautiful it almost hurts to look at you. Saying I don't know you— That's just crazy talk."

"You fell in love with a pretty face, but you don't know what's inside me. I'm not good and kind and oh, hell, saintly. I'm nothing like that. You might have been married to the saint, but the woman you want to ask to marry you now is the sinner."

"Why do you say that? What could you possibly have done that could be so bad?"

I was a prostitute. I sold myself for money.

If she told him, it would be the end. Couldn't she salvage something, anything of the relationship they had? How could she tell him the truth, and then see him every day at work and pretend it didn't matter to either of them?

"It doesn't matter. I can't marry you. You have to accept my decision."

"How can I? What kind of screwed-up decision is that, when we love each other?"

His eyes blazed. She knew he was angry and

could only pray his anger would push him away from her.

"It's the only one I can make. Marriage is out of the question. If you can't accept that, then we're done. We won't be able to have even a casual relationship, and if that happens it's going to make working together pure hell."

"You're serious. You're really serious about this."

"Dead serious."

"Then it's hell," he said, and left her.

CHAPTER TWENTY-ONE

By the time Jack got home Cole was in bed asleep. Good thing, because he wasn't ready yet to explain to his son what was going on. Hell, he didn't understand it, how could he explain it to Cole?

Ava loved him. She'd admitted it. But she wouldn't marry him. Not only that, she wouldn't even *consider* marriage. She'd had a total meltdown at the mere mention of the word. Her reaction made absolutely no sense to him.

Even so, he shouldn't have got angry, shouldn't have said they were done. Because he wasn't finished with her. He couldn't be until he'd at least tried to convince her that they could work through whatever problems she thought were an obstacle to their marriage. Assuming he could get her to tell him what she thought those problems were, of course.

Late the next afternoon he went to her house. She seemed surprised to see him but she let him

The hell of it was, he didn't know which would be worse to live with. Having that small part of her she chose to share or having nothing at all.

BY WEDNESDAY AFTERNOON Ava and Jack had been out on the bay twice. They'd spoken a combined total of about sixteen words to each other. Ava knew she should be glad he'd accepted her decision and that in time he would get over her and they'd both go on with their lives. But she also knew that while he might get over her, she would never get over him.

Still, there was nothing she could do now but go on with her work and bury herself in the study. Her work had sustained her through the years, it would do so again. Dolphins and dorsal fin images were a lot easier to deal with than people and failed love affairs.

Cole had made a lot of progress with converting the analog files to digital in a few weeks, but his time spent in the dolphin tank had cut into his work for her, so there was still plenty to do. Ava found herself working longer and longer hours in an effort to give herself something to do besides obsess about Jack, second-guess everything she'd done or said before coming right back to the same conclusion. She'd done what she had to do. No other choice had been possible.

She was in her office Thursday afternoon when there was a knock on her door. "Come in," she said, hating the hopeful lurch her heart gave every time someone knocked. It wouldn't be Jack. It never was.

"Could I talk to you?" Cole asked from the doorway.

"Sure. Come on in."

"I need to ask you something. Something, um, important." He stood close to the door, looking uneasy, as if he was ready to bolt any minute.

"Of course." When he didn't say anything, she prodded, "Is it about work?"

He shook his head.

"Would you like to sit down?"

Again, he shook his head but he did take a couple of steps forward. His hands clenched as he stood there uncertainly. "It's about my dad. About you and my dad."

He knew they'd broken up. Those were some of the few words she and Jack had exchanged Monday. Ava had asked, "Does Cole know?" and Jack had replied with "Yes." Then Ava had asked, "Is he all right with it?" and Jack had simply stared at her, saying nothing.

She'd got the message. If Jack was off-limits, so was his son.

"What about your dad and me, Cole?"

"He told me you broke up." Hesitating, he stuffed his hands in his pockets and looked terribly uncomfortable. "He said he asked you to marry him and you said no. He didn't tell me why you wouldn't. He said it didn't matter."

"It's…complicated."

Cole raised earnest, beseeching eyes to hers. "He's been real bummed about it. Way bummed. He doesn't say much, but I can tell."

She had to swallow the lump in her throat to say, "I'm sorry. I didn't— I don't want to hurt him."

He gnawed on his lip, then said with a rush, "Is it because of me? Because you don't want to raise someone else's kid?"

"Oh, Cole, no." She got up and went to him, laying a hand on his arm. "Of course I didn't break up with your father because of you. How can you think that?"

"Because if it is…" he continued doggedly "…in about two-and-a-half years I won't be around much. I'll be going to college. I know that sounds like a long time, but I swear I'll stay out of your way and—"

"Cole, stop it." Stop, before guilt completely destroyed her. "Please, don't do this." What was she supposed to say to a sixteen-year-old boy with his heart in his eyes? That he could even think for a moment he was at fault made her feel lower than algae on the bottom of an aquarium.

"Sit down. Please."

He took a chair and she sat in the one next to it. "My decision had nothing to do with you. It's not your fault in any way. I would feel honored to have you as a stepson. But your father and I, we just wouldn't suit each other." Which was a damn lie but needed to be said anyway.

Cole said nothing, just looked at her with those young eyes that saw through so much. She went on, "I can't marry your father, Cole. Not because of anything you've done, or anything he's done. He's a wonderful man. But I just...can't marry him."

For a long moment, he still didn't speak, he simply looked at her, his expression inscrutable. "Okay," he finally said, then he got up and walked out. Like his father, he knew when to make an exit.

Ava had the distinct impression Cole wasn't buying a word she said. Wonderful. She'd not only hurt Jack and herself, now she'd hurt Cole. She was beginning to regret she'd ever set foot in Aransas City. Yes, finding her brothers had been a miracle, reconciling with her mother even more so. But she'd also found, and lost, the love of her life.

She didn't think it was a very good trade-off.

"GOTTA TELL YOU MY FRIEND…" Mark said Friday night while sitting in Jack's den flipping through channels on the TV "…you look like crap." He took a sip of his beer and leaned back in his chair, waiting for a response.

The only proper response Jack could think of was *Up yours,* but he didn't bother to make it. "Don't you have someplace else to be? Like your own house, hogging your own damn remote instead of mine?" He gave him a sour look and drank some of his own beer.

"Nope. I'm fancy-free and all yours." Mark flashed him a grin that made Jack grit his teeth. "Cat and the kiddos went to her mom's. I got a reprieve because my wife wanted me to come over and find out the scoop from you."

"There is no scoop. Go home, Mark."

"Come on, Jack. I know you and Ava broke up. Cat got that much out of her before she clammed up. And both of you have been looking like you lost your last friend all week. Added to that, you two looked pretty cozy at Jay's house on Saturday. So what gives?"

"We broke up. Saturday night. End of story."

"I don't think so."

"Since when did you become such a woman, wanting to talk all the time?" He took another sip, wishing he could get drunk but since Cole was out with his friends he knew he wouldn't. One of the other kids was driving tonight, but Cole knew he could call his father if he had a problem. Therefore, Jack had to be responsible. Not that getting smashed would solve this problem anyway.

"Since we're talking about my sister…" Mark said. "I had the distinct impression you were totally gone over her."

"I was." He drank again and set the can down. "I am. Not that it matters."

"It might. Ava doesn't look too happy either."

Jack laughed bitterly. "I don't know why. She's the one who ended things." Looking at Mark, he jabbed a finger in his direction. "Your sister makes no sense."

Mark spread his hands. "That's a woman for you."

"Yeah." He brooded a minute before saying, "She admitted she loved me."

"Oh, yeah?"

"Yeah." He nodded, still trying to figure that one out. "I asked her to marry me. Did you know that?"

"No. She hasn't said much besides that you two broke up and she didn't want to talk about it."

"Now there's a news flash," he said sourly. "You know what she said when I asked her? No. She says she loves me but she absolutely refuses to marry me. Not only that, but she won't tell me why. Just no, period. Now I ask you, does that make a lick of sense to you?"

"Nope. But I don't know her very well anymore. She's had a whole life I know almost nothing about. I do know she's divorced. Is that the reason?"

"Who knows?" He rubbed his neck. "Maybe. But I don't really think that's it."

"Has she talked to you about the past?"

"Some. She told me about your father, and why she left." He shook his head, not wanting to think about that. "She's talked to me about the people who took her in, how great they were, how much she loved them. And she told me a good bit about her career, her life since then. A little, not much, about her marriage."

"But nothing about the time between when she left home and when the Vincents found her, right?"

"No, nothing. I think it must have been bad. Really bad. She told me she would never talk about it."

"She was fifteen years old, Jack. She spent over three months on the streets. It makes my blood run cold to think about what might have happened to her. Alone. Young, vulnerable. Prey for every sort of pervert who walked the streets."

You think I'm a saint but I'm the sinner, he remembered her saying. Was she referring to her time on the streets? What happened to her that was so traumatic she wouldn't even speak of it?

"You think this is all tied up with whatever happened to her during those three months?"

Mark nodded. "Yeah, I do. Don't you? Nothing else makes sense. Maybe if you could get her to tell you about it, then you might have a chance. She might open up to you. That's part of the problem right there. Ava's the most closed-off person I've ever known."

"She's a loner," Jack said. "Very much so."

His expression troubled, Mark looked at Jack. "Miranda wasn't closed-off. Anything but, at least to me. But I don't know the woman she's become. She's not a lot like the child I remember."

"You can't force someone to talk if they don't want to. Believe me, I've tried."

"Try again. Don't give up on her. For her sake as much as yours."

"How do you know I'll do any good? Until recently, you hadn't seen her in more than twenty years. You said yourself you don't really know her anymore."

Mark took a while to answer. "I want her to be happy, Jack. She deserves to be happy, and I think you're the one who can help her."

"I'm supposed to keep after her even though she told me to forget about marriage? To forget any serious relationship. You want me just to lay myself out there to be crushed?"

"Do you want her?"

"Yeah. Damn it. I do."

"Then go after her."

Jack's phone rang and he picked it up, glad for the distraction. Until he saw Caller ID. *Aransas City Police Department.* His mouth dried up as he stared at the display. Maybe it was a wrong number. Or they were calling to solicit donations. *Yeah, right, at ten o'clock at night?* "Jack Williams."

"Dad, it's me."

"Why did the Aransas City Police Department come up on my caller ID?" Please, God, let this be a mistake.

"I'm in jail, Dad. Can you come get me?"

CHAPTER TWENTY-TWO

"DAD, ARE YOU THERE?"

Jack found his voice, forced himself to repeat calmly. "You're in jail."

"Well, uh, it's like, I'm more *at* the jail. Not exactly *in* jail. They brought a whole bunch of us down here, but some of us were allowed to call our parents to come get us. So can you come down here and get me?"

Trying to focus, he brushed aside the double-talk. Jail was jail, in his opinion. "You want to tell me why you're *not exactly* in jail?"

"Um, yeah, but can we talk about it when you get here? Other people are waiting to use the phone."

Because the cops had taken their cell phones, no doubt. "I'll be there as soon as I can. And Cole, you'd better have a damn good explanation for this." He hung up and looked at Mark, unable to think of a thing to say.

Mark shook his head sympathetically. "That didn't sound good."

"No. Not good at all." He got up and went to the kitchen, with Mark following. "I have to go to the police station and get my son out of jail."

"Uh-oh."

"Of course, he's not exactly *in* jail. Just *at* the jail. Whatever the hell that means."

"Sounds like he got carted down there but they didn't charge him."

"I can hope, I guess." Jack opened the door and they walked out. "I'll see you later."

"Good luck," Mark said.

"Thanks. I have a feeling we're going to need all we can get."

He wasn't the only parent there. In fact, given the number of people standing in the central area as well as filling every spare corner of the small station house, he wondered if the cops had brought in the entire teenage population of Aransas City. Or at least the fifteen- to seventeen-year-old group, he thought, recognizing several of them.

A redheaded police officer stood in the center of the group of adults, waving her hand in the air. "Okay, let me have your attention please. The sooner I do this the sooner you folks can collect your kids and go on home."

He recognized Maggie Barnes as the officer who had stopped him with a warning for speeding on his second day in town when he'd whizzed through without realizing the speed limit had changed. He had thought she was pretty and knew she was nice since she'd let him off with a warning instead of giving him the ticket he deserved. Intrigued, he did some investigating, discovered she was single and thought about asking her out. Then Ava had walked into his life and he hadn't given another woman a thought since.

"Here's the situation," Maggie said. "We got a tip that there were some goings-on down on the beach involving minors. Bunch of rowdies whooping it up and partying. Disturbing the peace. When we arrived, we discovered alcohol and drugs were involved as well." She paused, but no one spoke. Afraid to, Jack suspected. He sure was.

"We also found that about half or more of the kids didn't know anything illegal was going on and were just there hanging out, listening to music and having a good time. But although we sorted things out at the beach, we don't have enough officers to allow us to wait on the parents down there and book the rest of them down here as well. So we just brought the lot of them back to the station house."

"Maggie, are you saying you arrested all of them for something only a few did?" a man called out.

"No sir, I'm not. That's exactly what I'm not saying. The kids you're here to pick up right now are the ones we believe weren't doing anything more than having a good time. Nothing illegal. At least, that's what we think."

Looking around at all of the parents, she paused to let that sink in. "Of course, some of them may know a little bit more than they're letting on, and I don't doubt some of them have had a sip or two of beer and maybe something else. But for the most part, these kids aren't the ones we're concerned with. So, they're free to go."

A buzz of conversation broke out. Maggie let it go for a few moments, then she held up a hand for silence. "But since I'm one of the arresting officers and it's at our discretion to book your sons and daughters if we have reason to believe they were doing something illegal, I'm going to give you some advice. If it was my kid, I'd be having a talk with him or her about illegal substances and the problems they can cause. Among other things, getting thrown in jail when you're caught."

Don't worry, Maggie, he thought. *We're going to have that conversation—again—whether Cole likes it or not.*

He finally saw Cole, looking young, scared and defiant all in one slouching package. "Uh, thanks for coming, Dad. I'm sorry you had to." He shifted. "I can explain."

"Good," was all Jack said as he headed for his truck. He didn't say anything else. A lecture like the one he planned to deliver was best kept for when he could concentrate on what he said and not on driving.

Cole tried to say something a time or two, but when Jack didn't answer, he lapsed into silence.

They walked in the house and Jack tossed his keys on the counter. Pointing at a chair at the kitchen table, he said, "Sit."

Cole sat. "Look, Dad, I know you're mad, but I didn't do anything wrong. You heard Officer Barnes. That's why they let us go."

"We'll get to that in a minute." Jack pulled out a chair, propped his foot on it. Leaning close to Cole, he kept his eyes on his son's face. "What were you doing at the beach?"

"There—there was a party. Some of us decided to go. The guys I was with wanted to go."

"Were there any adults at this party?"

Cole scowled. "No."

"No, what?"

"No, sir," he said his voice low.

"Did you know there wouldn't be adults there?"

Now he looked sulky. "Yes. Sir," he added reluctantly.

"We've had this discussion before. You're not supposed to go to unchaperoned parties for exactly this reason," he said, his voice rising as his anger did. He sucked in a breath and reminded himself to calm down. "So you knew and you chose to go anyway. Even though you knew if you got caught there'd be hell to pay."

"Yes, sir." He paused and added, "It was just a party, Dad. I didn't think it was a big deal."

"Did you smoke pot?"

"Officer Barnes said—"

"I know what she said," he snapped. "I'm asking you. Did you do any drugs?"

Cole shook his head.

"Did you drink anything?"

"No, sir." He met Jack's eyes and shrugged. "Yes, sir. A couple of sips of beer. But that's all, I swear."

Should Jack believe him? On one level, he did. And obviously, the cops had. But on another level, he remembered walking into his house and catching Cole and his friends in the act. He wanted to believe his son wasn't lying to him this time, but he just couldn't be sure.

"Am I grounded?"

Jack laughed humorlessly. "What do you think?" Cole looked away and he continued, "Yes, you're grounded. No car, no going out. After school you go straight to work, come straight home when you're finished. For a month, at least. I'm just not sure what else is going to happen."

Puzzled, Cole looked at him. "What do you mean, what else? Isn't being grounded enough?"

"Apparently not. That's what I did last time and look where we are now." He walked over to the cabinet, got a glass down, put a couple of ice cubes in it and turned on the tap. Sipping water, he considered his son.

"I don't see why you're making such a big deal out of it."

"Also what you said last time. Looks like we're back to square one."

"What does that mean?"

"I've been thinking I should have been harder on you. It would have been better for you if I had been. But there might be a way to fix that." He set his glass down and looked at Cole. "The first time this happened, I thought about sending you away to school. To military school."

Cole's mouth dropped open. "No way."

He had thought about it. Not seriously, but he'd considered it. And he wasn't serious now. Or not entirely. But he wanted to get through to Cole. Now, before he did something that really landed him in trouble.

"It's beginning to look like an option again."

Cole sat up, staring at him. "You never—you never said anything about that. You can't do this to me! I won't go! I won't!"

"You'll go if I say you have to go."

"I didn't even do anything wrong! I told you I didn't and you don't believe me! The cops believed me and my own father doesn't."

"Yeah, well the cops didn't walk in on you and your friends last spring. I did. And now this."

"I told you I wouldn't do it again and I haven't.

I wish I had, though. What difference does it make when you don't believe anything I say?"

"I don't know whether to believe you or not," Jack said honestly. "That's the problem. Once you've broken someone's trust it's hard to get it back."

Cole didn't say anything, just looked at him defiantly. Jack squeezed the bridge of his nose. Nothing like good old tension to do a number on your head.

"I think we've said all there is to say tonight. Go to bed, Cole. We'll talk in the morning."

Cole got up but didn't leave the room. "I'm not going to military school. There's no way I'm going and you can't make me. I'm sixteen, I don't even have to go to school anymore. I could quit tomorrow."

"Sure you could if you want a dead-end job with no chance of a decent career. High school dropouts aren't exactly at the top of the job market. And if you think I'm supporting you if you drop out, think again."

Cole walked out of the kitchen and a few minutes later Jack heard his door slam with a resounding bang. Great. Just great. He couldn't convince the woman he loved to marry him. He couldn't convince the son he loved to straighten up. He was nothing more than a total failure where the most important people in his life were concerned.

CHAPTER TWENTY-THREE

BELLS RANG. Ava couldn't imagine why, since she'd always thought of bells as a happy sound and the dream she assumed she was having was anything but happy. One more dream reliving the breakup. One more time she would wake in the morning, miserably aware that reality wasn't a bit better.

Groggily she forced open her eyes as the ringing continued. She realized the sound was her phone and reached for it, knocking it on the floor. She finally grabbed it up and put it to her ear. "'Lo."

"Ava, it's Jack."

She sat up and fumbled to turn on the light, blinking at the harsh glare. "Jack?" With one hand she knuckled her eyes. "Is something wrong? What are you doing calling me at—" she turned the alarm so she could read it. "It's 2:00 a.m." Two-thirteen, to be exact.

"I know. I'm sorry. I wouldn't have called but I'm—I don't know who else to call. I've called all his friends, woken up their parents, and he's nowhere."

She was fully awake now, listening to the despair in his voice. "Who's nowhere? You mean Cole? What's wrong? Isn't he at home?"

"No, he's gone. We had a fight and— Damn it, if I'd realized he'd leave home over it I'd never—" He broke off. "But that doesn't matter. I checked on him about one-thirty and he wasn't in his bed. I've been calling everyone I know. No one's seen him."

"Have you talked to the police?"

His laugh held little humor. "Oh, yeah. For the second time tonight."

"What—" She started to ask a question, but it was obvious Jack needed her with him, not hanging on the phone asking him futile questions. "Never mind. I'll be there as soon as I can get there."

"I didn't call to drag you out in the middle of the night. I just— I don't know, I thought he might have gone to you. I hoped he had."

Ignoring his protest, she went on. "I'm sorry, he hasn't called me. I'm coming over. In the meantime, start thinking of places he might be, besides his friends' houses. Any place the police might not think to look for him."

"You don't have to—"

"Jack. I'm coming," she said, and hung up.

Ava didn't say anything when he opened the door. She simply stepped inside and put her arms around him, felt his come around her and hold on tightly. For a long moment, neither spoke, simply taking comfort from holding each other.

"We'll find him," she finally murmured. "Don't worry, we'll find him."

"It's my fault," he said when he let her go. "I should have known better than to threaten him. I should have just grounded him and left it at that, but no, I had to go and make him think I'd send him away."

"First things first. I saw his car in the driveway. So he's on foot?"

"Yeah. He's not stupid. He'd know if he took the car I'd have heard him. Plus, it would be easy enough to find him in a vehicle. The cops could have put out a bulletin for it. But he must have thought of that."

"That was my next question. The police are looking for him, I take it."

"Yes. They're looking at the parks, the schools, the beach, places like that." His eyes lifted to hers. "The bus station. They called a few minutes after I talked to you, and no one's seen him. They haven't checked the airport yet, but they said they'd ask the Corpus Christi police to do so. But he doesn't have enough money for a plane ticket. At least, I don't think he does."

"That's good. It probably means he's still around here."

"Maybe. Unless he hitchhiked out of town."

Her heart froze at that thought. "He might have," she said carefully. "But I don't think you should worry about that until you've exhausted all the possibilities here. Besides, the police are much better equipped to deal with that than we are. Tell me, Jack, how bad was your fight?"

"Bad. As bad as we've ever had."

"What happened?"

He shoved an unsteady hand through his hair. "A bunch of kids were hauled down to the police station because a beach party got out of hand. Cole wasn't booked but I had to go get him. They said drugs and alcohol were involved, but they didn't think all the kids had been doing them. So they sent them home. But I..." His voice trailed off, then he said, "When I saw the police department come up on my caller ID, I knew it would be bad. But hearing that—I blew a gasket."

"That's understandable."

"Yeah, but— I didn't believe him. He swore he hadn't done anything, but I didn't believe him because last spring I caught him smoking."

A horrible thought struck her. "Did you— You said it was bad. Did you hit him?"

He shook his head. "No, of course not. The last time I spanked him he was four years old and had just run into the street. So, no, I didn't hit him. I did worse."

Thank God he hadn't hit him. She didn't know how she'd have stood that. But worse? What could be worse? "What did you do, Jack?"

"I threatened to send him to military school." He paced away, his steps jerky, running his hands through already disordered hair. "And the hell of it was, I didn't mean it. I couldn't do that, even if it were the best thing for him. There's no way I could send him away from me. Not now. I'm already depressed about him going away to college and that's not for two more years."

Two and a half, she thought, remembering her

conversation with Cole earlier that week. "But he believed you."

"Apparently." He made an impatient gesture. "Hell, yes, he believed me. I don't make idle threats. Not ordinarily. Of course he's run off. God, you'd think I'd learn."

"Beating yourself up isn't helping. I'm sure your reaction wasn't any different from a lot of fathers'."

"Their kids haven't taken off."

"Have you thought of any other places he might be? Here in town?"

He shook his head. "I've been racking my brain and coming up dry. When you said you hadn't seen him I decided to go driving around. It might be useless but I can't just sit here any longer."

Where could he be? Somewhere no one would expect to find him. "Wait a minute. There's a dolphin in rehab at the Institute. Cole's been helping take care of it."

"Yeah, I know. He's talked about it constantly." He looked at her, hope lighting his eyes. "You think he's gone to the Institute?"

"It's worth a try."

"But that dolphin's been on twenty-four-hour watch. There'll be all sorts of people with him.

Cole wouldn't go to the Institute unless he didn't care if I found him."

"Smiley's improved." Smiley was the name Cole had picked for the dolphin. "He was taken off the twenty-four-hour watch yesterday."

Jack's eyes blazed brighter. "That's it. It's got to be. Let's go."

"THANKS FOR COMING WITH ME," Jack said, on the way to the Institute. "I'm sorry I got you up. Sorry you're having to deal with this, too. But I really appreciate you being here."

Jack was driving, although Ava had offered to. She suspected driving made him feel a little less impotent, so she hadn't made more than a token argument. "Don't be silly. Of course I'm here. I'm worried, too. I— You know I care about Cole. Besides, you're a mess. You need someone with you."

"Do you think I'm overreacting?" His hands tightened on the steering wheel. "I mean, kids run away all the time, right? That doesn't mean they don't come back a few hours later, perfectly fine. Not all of them…leave town."

And never come back. She knew he was thinking of her childhood, though he didn't say it. "No, you're not overreacting." She was silent for a long moment, not wanting to say too much but needing to say something. "Bad things can happen to runaways. Trust me, I know."

He shot her a glance but she didn't say any more. There was no sense letting him know just how bad things could be for a child on his own.

"It kills me that he ran away. That he didn't trust me enough to even try to talk about it. I was going to talk to him tomorrow, when we'd both cooled off."

"He's young," she said. "Teenagers don't always make the best decisions. Especially when they're upset and scared."

"Is that what you did?" He pulled up to the Institute and turned off the truck.

"Yes." She gripped her hands together tightly in her lap. Thinking of what Cole might do tortured her. If he'd left town, if he was truly on his own… God, no, she wouldn't think of that.

"I made…a terrible decision. One I pray Cole won't ever have to make." She reached out, caught Jack's hand and squeezed it. "But I don't believe he will. My…situation was nothing like Cole's."

"No? You ran away from your father. Because

you were afraid of what he'd do. The same way Cole has."

"No, not the same at all. Even though he's angry and hurt, Cole knows you love him. You haven't abused him, haven't made him doubt his self-worth. You haven't made his life a living hell he'd do anything to get away from."

He looked doubtful. "No, but I've made mistakes. A lot of them."

"But you love him, and he knows that. It counts for more than you realize."

"What did you do, Ava? What happened to you that was so terrible?"

She glanced away. She wouldn't put that image in his head. Not with his son still missing. She wouldn't be that cruel. "You don't want to know. Not now, with Cole gone. But once we find him…" She left the rest unsaid, but she knew she'd have to tell him. Tell him and kill any hope for a future together. Not that she'd had any to begin with.

They got out and walked to the back door. Jack pulled out his key. "Do you know the alarm code?"

"Yes. Why, don't you?"

"I know it. But I don't know why Cole would."

"Has he stayed nights with Smiley and the other volunteers?"

"Some. Not all night, but pretty late some nights."

"Then he might know it, too. Open the door, Jack." Cole had to be there. She couldn't bear to think of what could happen if they didn't find him.

"IF HE'S HERE he reset the alarm," Jack said, punching in the code to disarm.

"If the night watchman made rounds, he'd have noticed the alarm wasn't on. It makes sense to reset it."

True, but would Cole have thought of that? They went inside, heading toward the back. Jack had never noticed how large the Institute was. Or how eerily quiet. But then, during the workday it wasn't quiet. He'd never been there at three o'clock in the morning.

The area that contained the rehabilitation tank was all the way at the back of the building, near the docks where the *Heart of Texas* was moored.

Turning into a long hallway, he saw the double doors leading into the rehab room. Thin beams of light showed through the cracks. The relief was crushing, until he realized it could still be someone else checking up on the dolphin and not his son at all.

Wordlessly, he looked at Ava.

"It almost has to be Cole," she whispered, reading his mind. "There weren't any cars in the parking lot."

Relief flooded back, intense and dizzying. "I hadn't thought of that," he said, just as quietly. He turned the knob and opened the door.

Cole sat with his back to them, on the edge of the huge tank, his feet dangling in the water. Dejection was in the slump of his shoulders. Smiley circled the perimeter, emitting sharp cries and tossing his head at the boy. Jack could have sworn the sounds were sympathetic, as if the dolphin understood what the boy was going through.

"Don't make me go to military school," Cole said without turning around. "I don't care what else you do to me, just please don't make me go."

CHAPTER TWENTY-FOUR

"I'LL LEAVE YOU TWO ALONE," Ava murmured, giving his hand a supportive squeeze. "Come to my office when you're ready to go home."

"Thanks." He walked over to the pool, took off his shoes and socks and rolled up his jeans. He took a seat beside his son, pondering what he wanted to say.

Cole's face was averted, only his profile visible, but Jack could see the tearstains on the one cheek presented to him. Those tear tracks reproached him, made him want to hold his son close, like he had when he was a little boy. Hold him tightly and tell him everything would be okay. But he couldn't do that anymore because he simply didn't know that everything *would* be all right.

"How did you know it was me?"

Cole hunched a shoulder. "I knew you'd figure

out where I'd gone. I mean, it's Aransas City. It's not like there are too many places to hide. But I couldn't think of anywhere else to go."

"It must have taken you a while to get here. It's five miles or more to our house."

"I ran most of it."

"Does that mean you're going to run track again, like you did in Galveston?"

Cole looked at him. "How can I if you send me to military school?"

"About that… You don't have to go to military school," Jack said. "That was just talk."

Cole's eyes widened in surprise. "Really? You were so mad, I thought you meant it."

"I wanted to get your attention. But I didn't want you to run away." They both watched the dolphin for a minute, then Jack said, "I've never told you about my college roommate. My first roommate."

"I thought you only went to college for a year."

"Two years. Then I got interested in fishing and I never finished. But I'm talking about my freshman roommate, a friend of mine from high school. He got into drugs, big time. I'm not sure how he got through the first semester without failing but by the second—when I'd moved in

with someone else—he wasn't even pretending to
go to class. He ruined his life, Cole. Destroyed it.
I heard he'd been in and out of rehab, but I lost
track of him after I quit college. I don't want that
for you, son. It terrifies me that I might lose you
to drugs."

"Dad, I'm not doing drugs. It really was just that
one time that I tried anything. I swear, I didn't
even really want to do it. They brought it over
and— I should have told them to forget it, but I
didn't."

Studying his son, Jack said, "I believe you.
But even if I didn't, I realized something after you
took off tonight. I can't be your conscience. I
can't always be around to make sure you're not
doing something you'll regret. I have to trust you
to make the right choices. But if you're going to
make the right choice, you have to be informed.
So I decided to tell you about my friend. I should
have done it before, the first time I caught you. I
don't know why I didn't."

"I made a mistake one time, Dad. I'm not
going to screw up again. Tonight wasn't my
fault."

Jack raised an eyebrow.

Cole grinned sheepishly. "Well, okay, going

to the party was my fault. But not the cops and everything."

"You're lucky they didn't throw you all in jail."

"Yeah, I figured that out. I'm sorry, Dad."

"Me, too." He put his hand on Cole's head and ruffled his hair, as he'd done since Cole was small. "Don't run off again, okay? I'm too old to be that scared. Next time, we'll talk it through." He got to his feet and, reaching out a hand, he helped Cole up.

"Dad, can I ask you something?"

"Sure."

"Am I still grounded?"

He laughed. "Afraid so, son."

"I kinda thought that would be your answer." But he didn't look too dejected about it.

"We'd better go get Ava. She's probably fallen asleep at her desk."

"Are you two back together? I mean, she came with you and all, so I just wondered."

She'd come through for him tonight when he'd needed her most. But he couldn't pretend there weren't still problems and a story she intended to tell him. A story he thought might finally explain why she wouldn't marry him. Regretfully, he shook his head. "I don't think so."

"Dad?" He looked at his son. "I wish you were."

"Yeah. I wish we were, too."

THE NIGHT BEFORE, when they had finally returned to Jack's house, they'd all been exhausted. Ava had suggested they postpone their talk until the following day and had told Jack to come to her place after lunch. He left Cole cleaning the garage. Jack figured since he was grounded he might as well be useful, too.

Ava let him in and offered him iced tea. "I'll have tea if you're having it." She didn't look like she'd slept well, but she probably hadn't got back to bed until after four, so that was no surprise.

Before she could leave the room he caught her hand. "Ava, wait. Last night Cole asked me if we were getting back together."

"What did—what did you tell him?"

"I told him I didn't think so. But Ava, if there's a chance for us, I want it."

Her eyes met his. "I know you think you do. Ask me that again, after you've heard what I have to say. If you still want to." Pulling her hand out of his, she left the room.

He looked around her house. It was spotless,

not a thing out of place. She was usually fairly neat, but not this neat. The place looked like she'd been cleaning for hours. He wondered if she'd even been to bed or had spent the rest of the night cleaning. To keep her mind off what was to come?

She took so long to bring the drinks he started to wonder if she'd left, but a few minutes later she brought them in and sat on the couch beside him.

He hated that she looked so distressed, so exhausted. He wanted to make it better, not worse. He didn't want her to talk if it would only cause her pain. "You don't have to tell me this unless you want to."

"Yes, I do." She picked up her tea and drank some before speaking again. "You deserve to know the truth. To know what kind of woman you think you've fallen in love with."

"I know the kind of woman I've fallen in love with."

"No, you don't, Jack." She hesitated, as if she wasn't sure how to begin. "I've never told anyone this story, except Jim and Jeri Vincent. I didn't tell my ex-husband, and that was part of our problem. I couldn't be honest with him. I can't be honest with anyone about my past."

He took a sip of tea and set down the glass.

"You haven't been dishonest. You said there were things that you couldn't—wouldn't talk about. That's not the same at all as being dishonest."

"Yes. Yes, it is. Just listen." She clasped her hands together and started. "I was fifteen when I ran away. I told you my father found me with my boyfriend and beat me." Jack nodded. "I didn't tell you what he called me, the whole time he was beating me. Whore. He called me a whore, over and over, and other words, worse words, words I didn't even know the meaning of."

Jack clenched his fist, wishing he could confront the man. "He was a sick bastard. You know that, don't you? No father should do that to a child." How could anyone beat a child they were supposed to love and protect? He thought of his own son and couldn't imagine it.

"But he did," Ava said. "I was afraid he'd kill me the next time, so I left." She sucked in a breath and added, "And I left my brothers at his mercy."

"There was nothing you could have done for them. You couldn't have protected them."

"That doesn't make it right that I left them. When I knew…what he might do to them."

Jack could think of nothing to say to that, but he reached for her hand.

Drawing back, she shook her head. "No, don't touch me. It's hard enough without that."

He withdrew his hand, wishing she would let him help her, comfort her. But she seemed determined to do this all alone. She acted as if…as if she were confessing to a crime. Maybe she was. From her behavior, he suspected it was bad, but he didn't know how bad.

"I stole money from my mother and took a bus out of town. To Memphis. I never made it there. I ended up in Pensacola. I'd been robbed of what little I had, so I was flat broke and scared to death I'd have to go home. I was afraid to try to get a job. They would know I was a runaway and they'd put me in the system. The system would send me home, and I couldn't risk that.

"For days I scrounged food out of garbage cans and at night I hid in the alleys. Finally, I met…someone. He caught me when I tried to pick his pocket. I thought he was drunk, and I could grab his wallet and get away." She smiled, briefly, bitterly. "Wrong. But instead of calling the cops, he took me to his apartment and fed me. A real meal, a sandwich and a soft drink. Even…potato chips. He said his name was Tyrone. Tyrone Presley," she said softly.

Jack was getting a sick feeling. He was afraid he knew what was coming and if it was what he thought— Oh, God, what had happened to her?

"He said I could shower and he'd get me some clothes. That he'd find me a place to stay. He knew of one not far from there." She cast her eyes toward the ceiling, gathering herself together, then continued. "I wasn't stupid. Oh, I was, but I thought I was so smart. Not naive at all." She laughed humorlessly. "But I was so hungry, and Tyrone was the first person to be nice to me since I'd been on my own. I decided I didn't care what he wanted from me. Even if he wanted sex, I didn't care. I asked him why he was being so nice to me. He just smiled." She shuddered. "I really grew to hate that smile."

Jack wanted to stop her. He didn't want to hear it. Didn't want to hear the horror in her voice, to hear about something that he couldn't change, couldn't fix, couldn't help. But he didn't say a word. As bad as it would be, he only had to hear it. Ava had been forced to live through it.

"He had sex with me that night. He wanted to make sure I wouldn't disappoint his clients."

Jack's stomach clenched, rolled. He didn't speak. He couldn't.

Totally expressionless, she looked at him. "That's how I became a prostitute. A whore, just like my father had called me. Only now I really was. Tyrone explained it to me. I'd get forty percent, he took the rest. Except it was really more like seventy-thirty. But you didn't argue with Tyrone. He made you sorry if you did."

She stopped, seemingly lost in thought. Jack had no idea what to say or how he was supposed to handle this. Finally he found his voice. "You were a child. You should have been protected from people like him."

She shrugged. "That's what happens when you live on the streets. Not a pretty story, is it?"

It was a brutal story. And terrifying, to think she'd lived that life. To know she had believed she had no other alternative. "This is why you won't marry me? Because of a mistake you made when you were a child? A desperate child? Why would you punish yourself for something you did out of desperation?"

"Because as sordid as it is, that's not the end of the story. It gets worse."

How could it get worse? Wasn't it already as bad as it could possibly get? He looked at her, and waited.

"After a couple of months, I got pregnant," she said flatly. "Father unknown. I pretended Brad, my boyfriend from home, was the father. Dreamed he'd come and rescue me. Marry me. Needless to say, that didn't happen."

Her laugh was the saddest sound Jack had ever heard. He couldn't stop from reaching for her hand and holding it. He didn't think she was aware of it. She was too lost in the pain of the past.

"Tyrone wanted me to get rid of it. I didn't want to. Realistically, I knew Brad wasn't coming. He didn't know where I was, and I couldn't—I couldn't call him. I don't know what I thought I'd do with a baby, how I thought I'd take care of it, but…I wanted it." She pressed her lips together. "Tyrone and I argued. I stood up to him, told him he couldn't make me. He could and he did. He took me to a friend of his who he said would fix me right up. Then I could go back to earning my keep like a good little whore."

"Oh, Ava. No." His heart twisted.

Her voice grew stronger, colder, her eyes more desolate, like a winter sky. "He fixed me, all right. I remember screaming, but no one cared. If they heard, they ignored it. Nobody crossed Tyrone. I was so scared, scared I would die. I almost did. I wanted to. It hurt… God, it hurt so bad." She bit her lip, took a breath. "I got sick. Infection set in. Tyrone dumped me by the E.R. Just drove by and shoved me out of the car, like trash. Jim Vincent was the doctor who took care of me. He saved my life."

Saved her life, and cost her… "That's why you had to have a hysterectomy, isn't it?"

Her smile was brief and bitter. "You guessed it. Appropriate, don't you think?"

Anger hit, swift and sudden. Not at Ava, but at everything that had conspired to make her live through that hell. "No, I don't. Why do you think you should be punished any more than you already have been? Isn't what you went through enough?"

"Haven't you heard anything I've said?" She got up and paced across the room before turning and facing him again. "Damn it, Jack, listen to me. This isn't a movie. It's real and it's ugly, uglier than you can imagine. I was a whore! A prostitute! I slept with men for money! And then I did worse. Don't tell me you're just fine with that, I won't believe you."

He got up and crossed the room to her. Gathered her hands in his. "You were a child. A desperate child who was preyed on by a monster. You were a victim, not someone who deserves to be punished."

She stared at him, her eyes wide with confusion. "You must…hate me. How can you not?"

"Nothing you've said, nothing you've done could make me hate you. I love you, I told you that. What you've just told me doesn't change my feelings."

"How can you love me? How can you, when you know the truth? You're not even shocked."

"I am shocked. And appalled that the lost child we've been talking about ever had to go through what you went through. It's horrible and, yes, shocking. But what you did doesn't put you beyond the pale, Ava. It shouldn't mean that you have to spend the rest of your life paying for a mistake you made when you were fifteen years old." He stroked her hair, pushed it back from where it fell in her face. "You deserve to be happy. Forgive yourself, Ava."

"I can't," she said, and turned away.

CHAPTER TWENTY-FIVE

"YOU CAN'T FORGIVE YOURSELF?" Jack said. "Or you won't?"

Ava turned to look at him. She'd just told him her dirty, sordid secret and he was looking at her not with disgust, but with...love.

"What's wrong with you? How can you even look at me now and not be disgusted?" And how could she forgive herself when what she'd done was unforgivable?

"Come sit down, Ava. We need to talk and there's no sense doing it standing here."

Still confused, she did as he said.

Once again, he gathered her hands in his, but this time he brought them to his lips and kissed them. "Did you think telling me this would drive me away?"

"Yes."

"It didn't drive the Vincents away. They knew everything and yet they adopted you."

"Y-yes. But they— That was different. They loved me. I don't know why."

He smiled. "Because you're very lovable. You just don't believe it." His thumb rubbed her knuckles, soothing, comforting. "It's a horrifying story, and it hurts me that you had to go through it. But it's over. It was over more than twenty years ago. I think you need to focus on what you've done since then."

"What I've done…since?" she asked blankly.

"You didn't let what happened, what you went through, destroy you, Ava. Not everyone could have gone on and accomplished what you've accomplished since the Vincents took you in. You finished school. You have a Ph.D., for crying out loud. That's something to be proud of along with the fact that you're well-respected in your field."

"I am proud of that, but—"

"I'm not finished. You've also reconciled with your brothers. You've forgiven your mother and are making a new relationship with her."

"None of that negates what I did. Nothing ever will."

"You made a mistake. What purpose does it

serve to continue to punish yourself? When you have so much right here, right now that could make you happy. You could make me happy, too. And Cole." He squeezed her hands, looked into her eyes. "I love you, Ava. Cole loves you. We want to be a family with you. All you have to do is let us."

"You—you still want to marry me?" He did. She could see it in his eyes.

He put his arms around her, kept his eyes on hers as he lowered his head and kissed her. His mouth moved slowly over hers, his tongue slipped through her parted lips, flicked inside and withdrew.

He pulled away and his smile held everything she'd thought was finished forever. Happiness. Most of all, love.

"I love you, Ava. Marry me."

"Are you sure?"

"I'm sure. But if you need more convincing, I'm willing."

She laughed. Her heart was bursting. "I feel…free. For the first time since I was fifteen, I feel free."

"Does that mean you'll marry me? Be my wife and let me love you?"

"Yes. I'll marry you, Jack." She kissed him to seal it.

THREE WEEKS LATER, she and Jack exchanged vows in the living room of his house. Cole stood up for him and Cat was her matron of honor. Their families had all made it, even her mysterious brother Brian. They'd asked Jared Long as well, who had generously given them both a week off so they could go on their honeymoon. Jack's parents had come from Colorado and were going to stay with Cole.

The house was overflowing with adults, children and two excited dogs who'd somehow managed to come inside and were currently under the dining room table searching for stray scraps of food.

"Happy?" Jack asked her. He had one hand on her waist and was feeding her bites of cake with the other.

"Delirious." She kissed him, then took a sip of champagne. "This is a perfect day."

"It will be even better once we start the honeymoon."

"Patience is a virtue," she told him, laughing. "Everyone went to so much trouble, we can't leave yet."

"They'll never notice," Jack said. "Everyone's eaten so much they're comatose." He looked around. "Except your brother Brian and my dad. They're out throwing the football with Cole."

"In their good clothes. Men are so strange." Jack grinned but didn't take that bait. "I can't believe Brian flew in from China. Although he told me he's coming back to the States for good now, once he finishes up his current job."

"Don't take this the wrong way but right now I have zero interest in your brother. Any of your brothers."

Her smile widened. "Oh? What do you have an interest in?"

"The honeymoon."

"Did anyone ever tell you that you have a one-track mind?"

"Yes. And right now every bit of it is on you." He put his arms around her and kissed her.

"The feeling is very mutual," she said, and kissed him back.

"OH, NO!"

The reaction slipped out before Emma Valentine could stop it, for there stood the very man she most wanted to avoid seeing again.

He didn't look any happier to see her.

"Well, come on, get on board," he said gruffly. "I won't bite." One eyebrow rose. "Though I might nibble a little," he added, mostly to amuse himself.

But she wasn't paying any attention to what he was saying. She was staring at him, taking in the royal blue uniform he was wearing, with gold braid and glistening badges decorating the sleeves, epaulettes and an upright collar. Ribbons and medals covered the breast of the short, fitted jacket. A gold-encrusted sabre hung at his side. And suddenly it was clear to her who this man really was.

She gulped wordlessly. Reaching out, he took her elbow and pulled her aboard. The doors slid closed. And finally she found her tongue.

"You…you're the prince."

He nodded, barely glancing at her. "Yes. Of course."

She raised a hand and covered her mouth for a moment. "I should have known."

"Of course you should have. I don't know why you didn't." He punched the ground-floor button to get the elevator moving again, then turned to look down at her. "A relatively bright five-year-old child would have tumbled to the truth right away."

Her shock faded as her indignation at his tone asserted itself. He might be the prince, but he was still just as annoying as he had been earlier that day.

"A relatively bright five-year-old child without a bump on the head from a badly thrown water polo ball, maybe," she said defensively. She wasn't feeling woozy any longer and she wasn't about to let him bully her, no matter how royal he was. "I was unconscious half the time."

"And just clueless the other half, I guess," he said, looking bemused.

The arrogance of the man was really galling.

"I suppose you think your 'royalness' is so obvious it sort of shimmers around you for all to see?" she challenged. "Or better yet, oozes from your pores like…like sweat on a hot day?"

"Something like that," he acknowledged calmly. "Most people tumble to it pretty quickly. In fact, it's hard to hide even when I want to avoid dealing with it."

"Poor baby," she said, still resenting his manner. "I guess that works better with injured people who are half asleep." Looking at him, she felt a strange emotion she couldn't identify. It was as though she wanted to prove something to him, but she wasn't sure what. "And anyway, you know you did your best to fool me," she added.

His brows knit together as though he really didn't know what she was talking about. "I didn't do a thing."

"You told me your name was Monty."

"It is." He shrugged. "I have a lot of names. Some of them are too rude to be spoken to my face, I'm sure." He glanced at her sideways, his hand on the hilt of his sabre. "Perhaps you're contemplating one of those right now."

You bet I am.

That was what she would like to say. But it suddenly occurred to her that she was supposed to be working for this man. If she wanted to keep the job of coronation chef, maybe she'd better keep her opinions to herself. So she clamped her mouth shut, took a deep breath and looked away, trying hard to calm down.

The elevator ground to a halt and the doors slid open laboriously. She moved to step forward, hoping to make her escape, but his hand shot out again and caught her elbow.

"Wait a minute. *You're* a woman," he said, as though that thought had just presented itself to him.

"That's a rare ability for insight you have there, Your Highness," she snapped before she could stop herself. And then she winced. She was going to have to do better than that if she was going to keep this relationship on an even keel.

But he was ignoring her dig. Nodding, he stared at her with a speculative gleam in his golden eyes. "I've been looking for a woman, but you'll do."

She blanched, stiffening. "I'll do for what?"

He made a head gesture in a direction she knew was opposite of where she was going and his grip tightened on her elbow.

"Come with me," he said abruptly, making it an order.

She dug in her heels, thinking fast. She didn't much like orders. "Wait! I can't. I have to get to the kitchen."

"Not yet. I need you."

"You what?" Her breathless gasp of surprise was soft, but she knew he'd heard it.

"I need you," he said firmly. "Oh, don't look so shocked. I'm not planning to throw you into the hay and have my way with you. I need you for something a bit more mundane than that."

She felt color rushing into her cheeks and she silently begged it to stop. Here she was, formless and stodgy in her chef's whites. No makeup, no stiletto heels. Hardly the picture of the femmes fatales he was undoubtedly used to. The likelihood that he would have any carnal interest in her was remote at best. To have him think she was hysterically defending her virtue was humiliating.

"Well, what if I don't want to go with you?" she said in hopes of deflecting his attention from her blush.

"Too bad."

"What?"

Amusement sparkled in his eyes. He was certainly enjoying this. And that only made her more determined to resist him.

"I'm the prince, remember? And we're in the castle. My orders take precedence. It's that old pesky divine rights thing."

Her jaw jutted out. Despite her embarrassment, she couldn't let that pass.

"Over my free will? Never!"

Exasperation filled his face.

"Hey, call out the historians. Someone will write a book about you and your courageous principles." His eyes glittered sardonically. "But in the meantime, Emma Valentine, you're coming with me."